## *Savannah Spectator* Blind Item

Expect this major announcement from a popular and powerful Senatorial candidate:

### I LEFT BEHIND A LOVE CHILD IN VIETNAM!

Could this mean the candidate in question is not quite as "honest" as his campaign would like us to believe?

Meanwhile Daddy's new little girl has been shacked up with the family security specialist, the manliest hunk of burning love this reporter would like to get her private eyes on! The question is: Is he keeping an eye on her for Daddy, or will Daddy come a-callin' for a good old-fashioned Southern shotgun wedding?

Dear Reader,

Welcome to another passion-filled month at Silhouette Desire. Summer may be waning to a close, but the heat between these pages is still guaranteed to singe your fingertips.

Things get hot and sweaty with Sheri WhiteFeather's *Steamy Savannah Nights,* the latest installment of our ever-popular continuity DYNASTIES: THE DANFORTHS. *USA TODAY* bestselling author Beverly Barton bursts back on the Silhouette Desire scene with *Laying His Claim,* another fabulous book in her series THE PROTECTORS. And Leanne Banks adds to the heat with *Between Duty and Desire,* the first book in MANTALK, an ongoing series with stories told exclusively from the hero's point of view. (Talk about finally finding out what he's *really* thinking!)

Also keeping things red-hot is Kristi Gold, whose *Persuading the Playboy King* launches her brand-new miniseries, THE ROYAL WAGER. You'll soon be melting when you read about Brenda Jackson's latest Westmoreland hero in *Stone Cold Surrender.* (Trust me, there is nothing cold about this man!) And be sure to *Awaken to Pleasure* with Nalini Singh's superspicy marriage-of-convenience story.

Enjoy all the passion inside!

*Melissa Jeglinski*

Melissa Jeglinski
Senior Editor
Silhouette Desire

Please address questions and book requests to:
Silhouette Reader Service
U.S.: 3010 Walden Ave., P.O. Box 1325, Buffalo, NY 14269
Canadian: P.O. Box 609, Fort Erie, Ont. L2A 5X3

# STEAMY
# SAVANNAH NIGHTS
## SHERI WHITEFEATHER

Silhouette®

Desire

Published by Silhouette Books
**America's Publisher of Contemporary Romance**

Special thanks and acknowledgment are given to
Sheri WhiteFeather for her contribution
to the DYNASTIES: THE DANFORTHS series.

To the eHarlequin.com community members on my
*Thief Of Hearts* and *Savannah Secrets* threads.
Thank you, all of you, for making those stories so much fun.

 SILHOUETTE BOOKS

ISBN 0-373-76597-5

STEAMY SAVANNAH NIGHTS

**Printed in U.S.A.**

## SHERI WHITEFEATHER

lives in Southern California and enjoys ethnic dining, attending powwows and visiting art galleries and vintage clothing stores near the beach. Since her one true passion is writing, she is thrilled to be a part of the Silhouette Desire line. When she isn't writing, she often reads until the wee hours of the morning.

Sheri's husband, a member of the Muscogee Creek Nation, inspires many of her stories. They have a son, a daughter and a trio of cats—domestic and wild. She loves to hear from her readers. You may write to her at: P.O. Box 17146, Anaheim, California 92817. Visit her Web site at www.SheriWhiteFeather.com.

# DYNASTIES: THE DANFORTHS

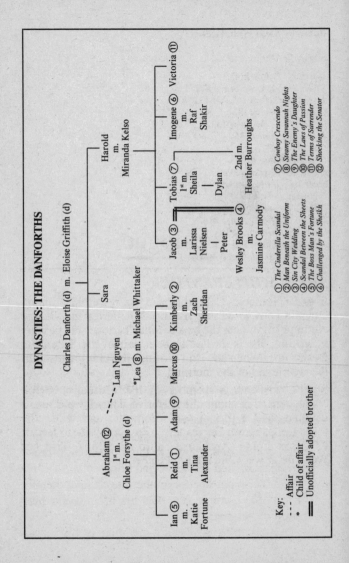

Charles Danforth (d) m. Eloise Griffith (d)

Sara

Harold
m.
Miranda Kelso

Abraham ⑫
1ˢᵗ m.
Chloe Forsythe (d)

Lan Nguyen
|
*Lea ⑧ m. Michael Whittaker

Reid ① m. Tina Alexander

Ian ⑤ m. Katie Fortune

Kimberly ② m. Zach Sheridan

Marcus ⑩

Adam ⑨

Jacob ③ m. Larissa Nielsen

Tobias ⑦ 1ˢᵗ m. Sheila
|
Dylan

2nd m. Heather Burroughs

Imogene ⑥ m. Raf Shakir

Victoria ⑪

Peter

Wesley Brooks ④ m. Jasmine Carmody

① *The Cinderella Scandal*
② *Man Beneath the Uniform*
③ *Sin City Wedding*
④ *Scandal Between the Sheets*
⑤ *The Boss Man's Fortune*
⑥ *Challenged by the Sheikh*
⑦ *Cowboy Crescendo*
⑧ *Steamy Savannah Nights*
⑨ *The Enemy's Daughter*
⑩ *The Laws of Passion*
⑪ *Terms of Surrender*
⑫ *Shocking the Senator*

Key:
- - - Affair
\* Child of affair
══ Unofficially adopted brother

# Prologue

*July 4th*
*Savannah, Georgia*

Security consultant Michael Whittaker remained on hawk-eyed alert. The fund-raiser was in full swing, and he'd been hired to protect Abraham Danforth, the man of the hour, the fifty-five-year-old widower running for state senator.

Michael, once a kid from the wrong side of the tracks, had earned his way to the top. His high-profile clients trusted and respected him.

In turn, he put his ass on the line to save theirs. But he didn't mind. That was his life's work, his chosen profession.

Along with hand-selected members of his security team, Michael had been acting as Danforth's personal bodyguard for months, after a female stalker, an unknown assailant Michael was still pursuing, had threatened the older man.

Assessing the activity in the Twin Oaks Hotel ballroom, he stood fairly close to Danforth. A small group of guests interacted with his client, while others mingled throughout the expansive setting, chatting amicably.

Michael shifted his attention to the petite brunette near the bar. She'd arrived late, keeping to herself. As far as he could tell, she hadn't spoken to another living soul.

Why? What was her agenda? Her expression proved difficult to discern, and that unnerved Michael. Normally he could read people. He possessed a sixth sense, a gut instinct that enabled him to see beyond the obvious, to get past the surface.

But everything about her mystified him: the creamy shade of her skin, the sleek dark hair fashioned in a ladylike twist at the nape of her neck, her exotic-shaped eyes.

Even her attire, a silky blue dress that flowed to her ankles, baffled him. The color was bold, as vibrant as a cobalt sky, yet she carried herself with understated elegance, with a soft, reserved nature.

She turned and caught his gaze, and for a moment, for one breathless instant, they looked at each other from across the room.

And that was when he saw the emotion she'd been masking, the flash of pain. She glanced away quickly, but the damage was already done. Suddenly Michael wanted to protect her, to hold her, to...

What? Kiss her? Cover her mouth with his?

Hell and damnation.

He cursed his hormones, the unwelcome blast of testosterone warming his blood. This wasn't the time to form an attraction, to get knocked off his feet.

The only female who should be occupying his mind was Danforth's stalker, and the lady in blue, that delicate little brunette, didn't fit the stalker's description.

As Danforth excused himself from the small circle of partygoers he'd been talking to, he glanced at Michael and motioned to a nearby terrace.

Apparently Danforth needed a short break. Michael shadowed his client, and together they stepped outside.

The terrace was empty, aside from a blonde seated on an ornate bench. Although she'd taken up residence in a dimly lit corner, Michael recognized Heather Burroughs—a polite, rather shy girl who worked for Toby Danforth, one of the politician's handsome young nephews, a single father who'd hired her as a nanny.

Michael knew Heather wasn't a threat to the Danforth clan. He'd checked out everyone employed by the family, including the new nanny. He'd even chatted with Heather earlier that night.

Respecting her privacy, he turned away and focused on his surroundings instead. The summer air was warm, the evening sky sprinkled with budding stars.

Just a short while ago, a fireworks display had lit up the night, cracking like thunder. The massive lawn and adjoining terraces, including this one, had been besieged with people. But things were quiet now.

As Danforth leaned against a columned wall, Michael stood near an empty doorway. And then he looked up and saw her. The brunette he wanted to kiss. The mysterious lady in blue.

Was it him or the man he'd been hired to protect that drew her near? That motivated her to follow them outside?

Danforth righted his posture, and Michael realized the brunette and his client were staring at each other. Did Danforth know her? Was she someone Michael should have been briefed about? Or did she have that mind-numbing effect on every man who locked gazes with her?

The politician snapped out of his trance. "I'm sorry," he said to her. "I didn't mean to be rude, but you bear a striking resemblance to someone I used to know."

The brunette blinked, and Michael suspected that Danforth's admission wasn't what she had expected to hear.

What the hell was going on?

"Was her name Lan Nguyen?" she finally asked.

"Yes. Yes, it was," the older man responded, a perplexed line creasing his brow. "How did you know?"

"Because I'm her daughter, Lea. *Your* daughter, Mr. Danforth, the child you abandoned in Vietnam."

Good God.

The father in question, the former Navy SEAL, couldn't seem to find his voice.

Concerned about a security leak, Michael moved forward and glanced in Heather's direction, motioning for her to keep quiet. She met his gaze and nodded, letting him know she hadn't intended to eavesdrop.

He acknowledged her compliance, then called his second-in-command, alerting his team to keep anyone else from coming onto the terrace.

Most likely, Heather could be trusted, but the last thing Danforth needed was a gossip-bound partygoer walking headfirst into this conversation. Or, heaven forbid, a reporter.

The Vietnam veteran hadn't denied the possibility that this mixed-blood beauty could be his daughter. Which meant what? That her claim could be true?

"Lan...survived?" The older man cleared his throat, the roughness breaking his voice. "She survived the attack on her village? I thought she was dead. I—"

"My mother is dead now," Lea interrupted, then teetered, swaying on her feet.

Worried she might faint, Michael reached for her shoulders, steadying her. He could feel her limbs vibrating, feel her weaving in his arms. "Hold on. Don't pass out."

"Take her home, Michael. Please, take her home." The request came from Danforth, who seemed genuinely concerned. "Stay with her until I contact you. Until we can sort this out."

Then to Lea, he said, "You can trust him. He won't hurt you."

She didn't argue, and neither did Michael. Much to his credit, Danforth did a damn good job of steeling his emotions. He returned to the fund-raiser under the careful watch of the security team, while Michael kept a trembling Lea by his side. He stopped briefly to speak with Heather, who made a solemn vow she would keep quiet. He thanked her, then escorted Lea to an inconspicuous exit.

Once they were in the limo, her tears began to fall. Without thinking, he covered her hand with his, promising everything would be okay.

But by the time he secured her address and got her home, he wasn't quite sure how to make everything okay. They entered her apartment, and she nearly collapsed, crying in earnest.

He reached for her, hugging her in the folds of his jacket, holding her against his heart.

"I thought it would be different," she whispered against his shirt, staining the starched white cotton with streaks of mascara. "I thought telling my father..." Her sentence trailed, drifting into nothingness.

She seemed so small, so fragile. Michael didn't know much about the post-war children who grew up as Amerasians in Vietnam, but he'd been called a half-breed for most of his life. And the derogatory connotation still twisted his gut.

She stopped crying, but he didn't let go. For nearly an hour, he rocked her, offering comfort.

Then something changed, and they became aware of each other's bodies, of his fly pressing her stomach, of being strangers locked in an intimate embrace.

She lifted her head and looked into his eyes. "I noticed you," she said.

He knew she was referring to the fund-raiser, to that instant in time, to the moment she'd revealed the ache in her soul.

He dried the moisture on her cheeks, tempted to taste the saltiness, to absorb her pain, to turn it into pleasure. "I noticed you, too."

"The way you're noticing me now?"

"Yes." He'd wanted to kiss her then, and he wanted to kiss her now. Desperately, he thought. More than words could describe.

# One

On Saturday afternoon, Lea answered her door, then stared at the man on the other side.

Michael never visited her at this hour. He never arrived at her apartment during the day, yet the Savannah sun blazed bright and hot, framing him in a warm glow.

He looked incredible, with his dark hair and dark eyes, his square-cut jaw and stunning cheekbones. His shirtsleeves, she noticed, were rolled up to his elbows, but his trousers were pressed to perfection. Michael Whittaker, the CEO of Whittaker and Associates, possessed a conflicting charm: rough yet polished, right down to the slow, Southern drawl.

A voice that sent naked shivers down her spine.

Nervous, she smoothed her blouse and wondered

what had prompted him to stop by. Did he want sex? Would he sweep her into the bedroom? Run those skilled lover's hands all over her body?

"Afternoon," he said.

"Hello." She looked past him and saw a shiny black Mercedes parked on the street. Was that his car?

Lea had been sleeping with Michael for the past month, yet she didn't know what kind of vehicle he drove. Somehow that made her feel cheap, like a bar girl in Vietnam.

Would he discard her after their secret liaison ended? Forget she existed?

She shifted her gaze from the car to the man and then considered touching him, wanting to smooth the lock of hair that slipped onto his forehead. The midday light cast a slight auburn sheen to the dark-brown strands, something she hadn't been aware of before.

But why would she? This was the first time she'd seen him standing in the sun.

"Aren't you going to invite me in?" he asked.

She blinked and nodded. He wasn't a vampire, although up until now, that was how she thought of him: her midnight fantasy, her forbidden lover, the tall, dark shadow who took her breath away.

On the night of the fund-raiser, she and Michael had ended up in bed, touching and kissing and making emotion-drenched love. Much to her surprise, he'd returned the following evening for more, until a month of hot, lust-driven nights went by.

And now, here he was in broad daylight—

"Lea?"

"What? Oh, yes." She stepped back, realizing she'd been blocking his entrance.

He strode to the center of her living room, his hands tucked in his pockets. She couldn't read his body language. Michael wasn't the sort of man a woman could predict.

Should she offer him a drink? Lea honestly didn't know what to do, how to react to his presence. When he arrived at night, the scenario played out like a naughty dream. She would open the door, and he would take control. Without words, without false pretenses, he would start the fantasy, thrilling her with his imagination.

Sometimes he led her to the bedroom. And sometimes he stripped her where she stood and dropped to his knees.

"Lea?" He said her name again, and her face went hot.

Was she blushing?

"Are you all right?" he asked in that spine-tingling drawl.

"Yes, I'm fine."

"I saw the paternity test results."

He met her gaze, and her heartbeat staggered. She shouldn't be having an affair with her father's bodyguard, with the security consultant hired to protect him. "Then you know for certain that Abraham Danforth is my father."

He cocked his head. "Yes."

"Is that why you're here? To convince me to speak with him?" After the fund-raiser, she'd agreed to take the paternity test Danforth's attorneys insisted upon. But even so, she refused to form an alliance with the former Navy SEAL who'd sired her. Of course, she couldn't explain why, especially to Michael.

"I'm not here on Danforth's behalf." He reached for the oversize seashell on her glass-topped coffee table, studied it and set it back down. Next, he assessed the drawings she collected, the sketches from sidewalk artists on River Street. She kept her bungalow-style apartment furnished with items that reflected the local culture, with no reminders of home, no painful memories of Vietnam.

"Will you stay with me, Lea?"

Her pulse jumped. "Stay with you?"

"For a few weeks. At my house."

"Why?" was all she could think to say. "Why are you inviting me to your home?"

"So we can get to know each other better." He moved a little closer, but he didn't touch her. "So we can spend more time together."

It was a compelling offer. Mystifying. Exciting. But Lea knew she should refuse.

She toyed with the barrette confining her hair. "I have to work. I'm not on a holiday."

"Neither am I. But that doesn't mean we can't have an adventure. Visit some clubs, go out to dinner, walk along the shore. Get to be friends."

Her reserve wavered. She wanted Michael's respect, his friendship. But did she deserve it?

"Well?" he asked, a smile playing on his lips and crinkling the corners of his eyes.

"Yes," she finally said, anxious to be near him. "I'll stay with you for a few weeks."

"Good." He smiled again, then gave her directions to his house and told her to meet him there at five o'-clock.

When he turned and headed for the door, he left her in a daze.

She watched him walk to the shiny black Mercedes, flick the electronic lock, get behind the wheel and drive away.

At least she knew what kind of car he drove, she told herself, as she rummaged through her clothes and fretted about what to pack.

Michael left Lea's house and proceeded to Crofthaven, the impressive mansion and estate her father owned.

He took the paved drive to the gate, the path flanked by magnificent moss-draped trees. Southern beauty at its finest, he thought, cursing to himself.

He was deceiving Lea, and now he was about to deceive Danforth, as well.

But what choice did he have?

Michael arrived at the columned mansion, a historical landmark built over a century before. Crofthaven boasted prestige and charm, as well as its own tragic ghost.

A member of the household staff ushered him into the sprawling entryway, where he opted to wait for his high-profile client.

Moments later, Abraham Danforth descended a spiral staircase. He was new to politics, but he had the kind of charisma that bolstered his squeaky-clean image. So much so, the media had dubbed him Honest Abe II.

Danforth decided to conduct their meeting in the garden, a location that provided plenty of privacy. They took up residence on a marble bench, summer blooms flourishing around them. Beyond the garden, a peach orchard scented the air. But the peaceful surroundings didn't pacify Michael's nerves, didn't make this meeting any less stressful.

"What's on your mind?" Danforth asked. In spite of the temperature, he looked cool and composed in pale gray trousers and a short-sleeve designer pullover.

Michael wasn't faring quite so well. A line of sweat trailed down his back. The hot August day would develop into a hot August night. And heated nights had become his obsession. As well as his downfall.

Because of Lea.

"There's something I have to explain." Feeling like a traitor, he met the older man's gaze. No matter how he tried to justify his behavior, bedding Danforth's daughter wasn't a gentlemanly thing to do. "Lea and I are—"

"Are what?" the politician prodded.

"Involved."

One eyebrow lifted. "How involved?"

"We're lovers," he responded, as honestly as he could. "And she's going to stay with me for a few weeks. So I'll be working a light schedule. My security team will continue to provide protection for you, but I probably won't be available."

Danforth squinted in the sun. "When did all of this occur?"

Michael knew he meant the affair. "It started that first night. I didn't intend to be with her, not like that. But we were attracted to each other, and..." He let his words trail. He wasn't about to admit that sex was all he and Lea had in common.

For the past month, they barely talked, barely communicated beyond a primal level, beyond late-night hours of passion.

"That first night?" Danforth stared him down. "I asked you to take her home and you slept with her? I entrusted you with her safety."

"I know. I'm sorry." He paused, keeping his emotions in check, the tightness in his stomach, the confusion Lea stirred. "But she needed me. And I needed her. Sometimes these things just happen."

"Yes, I suppose they do," Danforth responded, his tone quiet.

Michael nodded, realizing the other man wasn't going to press the issue any further. But why would he? The widower was burdened with his own brand of guilt. He'd been married when he'd made love with Lea's mother. An affair that resulted from a war-related injury and a bout of amnesia, but an affair just the same.

Although the media hadn't caught wind of it, Danforth wanted to come clean, to schedule a press conference and introduce Lea to the world, but she refused to have anything to do with him.

"I wish things would have turned out differently," Danforth said. "I never meant to leave Lan behind."

"I know." But Lea's mother was dead now, Michael thought. It was too late for Danforth to apologize to her.

Honest Abe's honesty only took him so far.

As the politician lapsed into silence, Michael pondered his recent suspicion, his belief that Lea might be the stalker he'd been tracking.

Yes, Lea. The woman he seduced almost every night.

She didn't fit the stalker's description, but she could have altered her appearance. And she was a computer analyst, more than capable of sending threatening e-mails and writing the virus that had crashed her father's computer several months before.

But he wasn't about to reveal his suspicions to Danforth. Not until he knew the truth.

The older man shifted his weight. "Why won't Lea give me a chance?"

"I don't know. She's still hurting, I guess." Michael couldn't speak for Lea, which was exactly why he'd invited her to his home. He needed to spend some time with her, to get to know her on a deeper level. To prove, he hoped, that he wasn't sleeping with the enemy.

Michael lived on a private street. A brick wall and an electronic gate encompassed the perimeter of his property.

Lea stopped at the intercom and announced her arrival. Once she was permitted onto the grounds, she followed a tree-lined driveway to an impressive two-story home.

She parked her car and Michael came out of the house wearing jeans and a T-shirt, his hair combed casually away from his face. His feet were bare and instantly she was reminded of her childhood, of the place she'd left behind.

"Is your luggage in the trunk?" he asked.

She looked up at him. He stood nearly a foot taller than her, with broad shoulders and long, lean muscles. "Yes, it is."

"Will you flip the lock?"

"Of course." She met his gaze, but she couldn't decipher the emotion in his eyes. But she never could, not even when they were in bed.

He removed her suitcase. He was a passionate man, an erotic lover, but he was complicated, too. Sometimes he smiled and sometimes he seemed stern. She suspected that he kept his true heart hidden. But she did that, too.

They approached the door and she stalled.

"What's wrong?" he asked.

"Nothing." She glanced down, debating what do about her shoes. He watched her, making her self-conscious. She decided to leave things be. She'd worked hard to shed her Vietnamese habits, to become an American woman. And women in the states didn't remove their shoes before entering a home. Instead, she took extra care to wipe her feet on the Welcome mat.

They entered the great room, where expansive windows offered a tidal marsh view. "Your home is exquisite," she said. The architectural detail included oak cabinetry, stucco walls and a massive skylight.

"Thank you. It's totally secure, with a state-of-the-art security system. The exterior is equipped with intrusion sensors. It was designed with my clients in mind." He gestured broadly. "Sometimes they stay here when they're avoiding the media. Or taking refuge from personal threats."

"You created a fortress."

"Whittaker and Associates protects high-profile clients."

"Like my father."

He nodded, and they both fell silent.

She glanced at the fireplace and noticed the stonework was inlayed with chunks of coral. The furnishings were white, with turquoise-colored accents. He'd spared no expense to make his home into a showplace. "Has my father ever stayed here?"

"No. He's well protected at Crofthaven."

She knew the name of Danforth's mansion, the place where his other children were raised. Lea could never be like her half siblings. They were blue bloods, born into a prestigious American family. She was *my lai*, an Amerasian born on the fringes of Vietnamese society.

"Let me show you to your room." Michael reached for her suitcase. "It's upstairs, just down the hall from the master bedroom."

They ascended an oak staircase and she followed him into an elegant suite, with wood floors and a four-poster bed. Glass doors led to a balcony overlooking a private dock.

"This is beautiful." The walk-in closet was far too big for her simple belongings and an adjoining bathroom provided a sunken tub and a separate shower. Lights framed a vanity mirror. "I'm humbled."

"It's the most feminine suite in the house."

"It's more than I imagined. Thank you." Would he visit her later? Slip into her room? Stay the night? Although they were lovers, they'd never awakened in each other's arms. Michael always left her apartment before the sun came up. Lea longed to cuddle with him, to bask in the afterglow of their lovemaking, but she wasn't brave enough to tell him that.

He placed her suitcase on a luggage stand. "Come on. I'll show you the rest of the house."

He led her down the hall, and his room left her speechless. She wandered around the suite, taking in every piece of furniture, every carefully thought-out detail. Even the bathroom was gorgeous, providing his and her sinks and a cedarwood sauna designed for a couple.

"Do you plan to get married someday?" she asked.

"Yes, but I'm not searching for a wife." He shifted his stance. "I'm hoping the right woman will come along."

She tried to picture his future bride. A tall, slim blonde, she decided. A lady who wore fashionable clothes and hosted Southern parties, making use of his extraordinary home. "Do you want children?"

He nodded. "Do you?"

She glanced away, wishing she hadn't started this conversation.

"Lea?" He pressed.

She adjusted her purse strap, pushing it farther down her shoulder, keeping it from rubbing against her neck like a hangman's noose. She was having an affair with Michael because she needed the closeness his body provided, the comfort of his touch. Dreaming beyond that was dangerous. But she dreamed just the same. "Yes, I want children. And a husband who loves me." A husband who wouldn't judge her, a husband she could tell her secrets to.

"I want that, too. With a wife, I mean. I want the kind of marriage my parents didn't have."

"They were unhappy?"

The muscles in his face tightened. "All they did was fight. Scream and curse at each other."

"I'm sorry." She'd assumed he'd been reared in a respectable environment. "Children should be nurtured. They shouldn't be subjected to anger."

"Or pain," he said, smoothing a lock of her hair, leaving a lump in her throat.

After an awkward beat of silence, he escorted her from his room. They went downstairs and he gave her a tour of the ground floor. An eight-hundred-square-foot gym led to a landscaped yard and a gazebo-framed hot tub. The game room was equipped with a pool table, air hockey and a jukebox. A wet bar offered sodas and spirits.

"You live well," she said.

"It keeps my clients entertained."

What about his lovers? she wondered. How many other women had he invited to his home?

"What's in here?" she asked, as they passed a closed door.

"Surveillance monitors. It's a security office."

She nodded and moved on, not wanting to steer the conversation in that direction.

Michael offered her a casual meal, and they spent the rest of the evening eating sandwiches and talking about inconsequential things. At bedtime, he walked her to her room.

They stood in the doorway, gazing at each other. She couldn't think of anything to say. She could smell the faded scent of his cologne, a woodsy fragrance that made the moment even more intimate.

He touched her cheek, and her knees went weak. She tried to keep her breathing steady. She didn't want him to know how nervous she was.

He caressed her face with the back of his hand, and her heart pounded much too hard. He didn't kiss her, but she didn't expect him to. He would come back later, she thought. When her room was dark, when moonlight dappled the bed.

He dropped his hand, but his eyes were still locked onto hers. "Good night, Lea."

"Good night, Michael."

Tall, dark Michael. She watched him head toward the master bedroom. He still wore jeans and a T-shirt, and his feet were still bare.

She closed her door and suddenly she panicked. She didn't want to need him this badly. She didn't want to lie in bed and wait for him. But by the time she bathed and climbed into bed, the sheets enveloped her in anticipation.

Had Michael bathed, too? Would his hair be freshly washed? Would the damp strands trail water over her breasts? She could almost feel him leaning over her, lowering his mouth.

Lea glanced at the clock, anxious for her lover.

But as the night wore on, as the moon slipped behind the trees and disappeared into a void of darkness, she found herself alone, waiting for a man who never came.

# Two

Lea entered the kitchen the following morning, trying to keep her emotions under control. Michael was at the stove, scrambling eggs. He looked up from the pan, and she couldn't seem to find her voice to greet him in a casual way.

He spoke first. "I gave my housekeeper a few weeks off. I thought it would be easier for us to be alone."

Why? she wondered. Why did it matter if they were alone? If he didn't intend to be with her, to treat her like a lover, there was no reason to hide their relationship.

"Did you get a good night's rest?" he asked.

Lea merely stared at him. She hadn't fallen asleep until dawn, and the sun was too bright on the window shades, too cheerful for a woman whose vampire never appeared. "I was restless."

"Me, too. Maybe we'll sleep better tonight." He turned off the flame and steered the conversation in another direction. "I hope you can stand my cooking. Madeline usually fixes meals for my guests."

Lea couldn't help but wonder why he hadn't slept well. "Madeline is your housekeeper?"

"Yes. She and her family live nearby. She's been a trusted employee for years."

"I don't mind cooking. I took culinary classes in college." And she knew how to make all sorts of American dishes.

"Good." He reached into a cabinet and removed two plates. "I'll hold you to that. But for now, we'll have to survive on my efforts."

She moved forward to take the china. She assumed they would eat breakfast in the morning room, a cozy enclave located off the kitchen.

His hand touched hers in the exchange. "You look pretty, Lea."

"Do I?" She'd brushed her hair until it shone, allowing it to fall freely to her waist. Her flower-printed dress was made of summer cotton, with thin straps and a simple bodice. She'd chosen sandals for her feet.

"You always look pretty." Although his expression gave nothing away, his words remained kind. "Sometimes I think about the fund-raiser. About how easy it was to notice you."

She clutched the plates to her chest. She could almost hear her heart pounding against them, making a clanking sound. "I noticed you, too."

"Of course you did. I was your father's bodyguard."

"You still are."

"Not for these next few weeks. I told him I was working a light schedule. That my staff would be providing protection for him."

"Why? So you could spend more time with me?"

He snared her gaze. "Yes. That's exactly why."

She wished she could admit that she'd waited for him last night, but she wouldn't dare. She wasn't about to embarrass herself.

Five minutes later, they sat across from each other at a wrought-iron table, the sun filtering through the blinds. Besides the eggs, he'd fried a platter of ham and toasted wheat bread. The coffee was bitter and dark, but Lea preferred tea.

"I forgot the orange juice." Michael went back into the kitchen and returned with a plastic carton. He poured the juice into Lea's glass. "I can tell you don't like the coffee."

She looked up. "I'm sorry. I don't drink much coffee."

He smiled a little. "I'll have to make a note of that in your file." He moved his fingers in the air, typing on an imaginary keyboard. "Lea doesn't drink much coffee."

He didn't really have a file on her, did he? She glanced at his mouth, at the slight tilt of his lips. He must be teasing her. "You sound like a cop."

"I was an MP." He scooped a second helping of

eggs onto his plate. He'd scrambled enough to feed an army. "Military police."

"I assumed that's what you meant."

"I've always been a law-and-order type of guy." He leaned forward, his smile gone, his gaze much too intense. "Being a security specialist suits me."

She tasted the ham, chewing carefully, trying to appear more relaxed than she felt. Whenever his features turned hard, whenever his eyes went dark, he seemed ruthless. Maybe he did keep a file on her, notes about the anxious woman who'd waited for him last night.

"I'm an investigator, too," he said. "I'm investigating a case for your father."

Lea's pulse skyrocketed, hammering horribly at her throat, throbbing at her temples. Had Michael been hired to find the woman who'd threatened Abraham Danforth? To bring her to justice? "I don't want to talk about my father."

"Why not?"

She gripped her fork a little harder, hoping her hand didn't tremble. "He abandoned me and my mother."

Michael's voice gentled. "He didn't mean to. He thought Lan was dead."

"I know. He told me that on the night of the fund-raiser."

"Then why won't you give him a chance?"

Because her guilt wouldn't permit it, she thought. Because it was safer to stay away from Abraham and his family.

She looked across the table at Michael. Did he

suspect her? Had he invited her to his home to keep an eye on her?

No, she thought. No. She'd been cautious, covering her tracks. The evidence wasn't supposed to lead in her direction.

"You have no right to do this," she said.

"Do what? Convince you that your dad is a decent guy?"

Lea didn't respond, so she and Michael finished their breakfast without finishing their conversation. She helped him clear the table and load the dishwasher. When he glanced at her, his expression grim, she struggled with her conscience. At one time, she'd believed that her vengeance was just, that she had a right to hate her father. But now she wasn't so sure.

"I have to unpack," she said, finding an excuse to retreat to her room, to hide from the shame of threatening Abraham Danforth, of deceiving his bodyguard, of wishing that Michael would wrap her in his arms and wash her sins away.

Michael checked his watch. How many hours was Lea going to avoid him? It was noon and she still hadn't emerged.

He sat in his home office, sorting through his notes about Lady Savannah, the woman who'd been threatening Danforth.

Troubled, he leaned back in his chair. Did Lea fit Lady Savannah's profile?

Yes, he thought. She did. But he couldn't condemn her without proof. What if he was wrong? What if Lea wasn't the stalker? What if she hadn't sent those cryptic e-mails? Or crashed her dad's computer? Or given herself the name Lady Savannah?

He put the file away and went upstairs to knock on her door. She answered, seeming lost, vulnerable—much too fragile, with her delicate bone structure and slim curves. He wanted to hold her, but touching her would only complicate his dilemma, making it worse.

The four-poster bed caught his attention, and he frowned at the mahogany posts and peach-colored duvet cover. He'd had every intention of stealing into her room last night, of making love to her, but he'd paced his quarters instead, fighting the urge.

How could he continue to sleep with her? With a woman he suspected of a crime? How could he use her for his own pleasure, then cast her aside if she were Lady Savannah?

"I'm sorry I upset you at breakfast," he said, moving farther into her room.

"I'm sorry, too." She sat on the edge of the bed and smoothed the front of her dress. The feminine fabric fit her graceful style and so did the backdrop of pillows, the romantic display of ribbon and lace. "I overreacted. I blamed you for being loyal to my father. But that isn't fair. You wouldn't work for a man you didn't trust."

"No, I wouldn't. But that doesn't mean Danforth is a saint. From what I understand, he was an absent father to the rest of his children, too. After his wife died, he pawned them off on other people. Relatives, nannies, au pairs, whoever was available. And then there were the boarding schools."

She seemed surprised. "I assumed he was close to his other children."

"I think he's trying to make amends with them now that they're grown."

"He's running for state senator. Maybe he's worried about his image." Thoughtful, she paused. "Maybe that's why he's taken an interest in his family. Why he's willing to accept me."

"That's possible, I suppose. But I think it's more than that."

"How can you be sure?"

"I've got a knack for figuring people out." But not Lea, he thought. She baffled him. When she bent her head, the gesture made her seem younger than her twenty-seven years.

Finally, she looked up and their eyes met. She had beautiful eyes, exotically shaped, with a sweep of thick, dark lashes. He wanted to cup her face, to kiss her, to forget that she was a suspect. But he knew he couldn't.

"Do you really have a file on me, Michael?"

"Yes, but I was just kidding about the coffee earlier." He sat next to her. "The day after the fundraiser, I started a background check on you." Something he refused to apologize for. "I had to. It's part of my job."

"Because you slept with me?"

"Because you claimed to be Danforth's daughter, and he's my client." He'd given Danforth information about her, facts he'd uncovered. Of course, Michael hadn't suspected her of being Lady Savannah then. Now he analyzed those facts in a different light. "Your file is mostly government documents. Your immigration papers, things like that. I'll show it to you if you'd like." But he wouldn't show her Lady Savannah's file. Not yet.

"Is there a copy of the paternity test in my file?"

"Yes. But Danforth gave it to me. It was sent to him, just as it was mailed to you."

For a long, drawn-out moment, they didn't say anything else, making his investigation seem like a sham. But deep down, he knew it wasn't. His suspicions were valid.

"Tell me about your childhood," he said. "About growing up in Vietnam."

"What good will that do?"

"How else am I going to get to know you?" He tried to picture her, a little girl living in a war-ravaged country. "To understand what you've been through?"

She reached for a pillow and hugged it. "My past isn't important."

"You were born after the fall of Saigon, after the U.S. withdrew." He rose from the bed, putting a physical distance between them, stopping himself from touching her, from feeling too much. Already he wanted to hold her, to give comfort. "You were a child of the enemy. That couldn't have been easy."

"Some of the women who had babies like me threw them away." She cradled the pillow as though it were an infant. "But my mother tried to protect me."

"She loved you."

"And I loved her. But it wasn't enough."

He thought about his family, about the shame of being gossiped about, of watching neighbors turn away in disgust. "Were people cruel to you?"

She went still, the ceiling fan above her head stirring her hair, feathering the long, loose strands around her face.

He remained near the window, watching her, studying her features, the ethnicity she couldn't deny.

"Other children used to throw rocks at me," she finally said. "Taunting me with an ugly *my lai* rhyme. But their parents didn't care. No one reprimanded them. It was like that from the beginning, from my earliest memory." She paused to take an audible breath. "My mother was treated badly, too. Like a whore. I was glad to leave Vietnam."

"And now you're in the land of the free." But was she any happier? Had she moved on with her life? Or was she still trapped within her grief, blaming Danforth for her pain?

Michael knew Lea had come to America through the Amerasian Homecoming Act, an act that allowed Vietnamese Amerasians and specified members of their families to enter the U.S. as immigrants. "I obtained copies of your records from the Philippine Refugee Processing Center." The refugee camp where she'd lived, he thought. Where the government had sent her before she'd come to America.

She cradled the pillow again. "It would have been easier if I wasn't alone. If my mother had been with me."

Michael nodded. Lan had died soon after Lea's

eighteenth birthday, the year her application had been processed.

"I worked hard in the PRPC classes," she said. "I wanted to learn English, to speak like an American."

"And you do."

"Like someone who was born here?"

"Yes. Very much so." And that had been her intention, he realized. Once she'd arrived in the States, she must have spent years perfecting the language the PRPC had taught her, losing the Asian inflection in her voice, listening to Americans, mimicking their gestures and casual phrases.

She looked up at him. "I wish I could talk like you."

He couldn't help but smile. "You lived in California. I was born and bred in Georgia."

"I could practice." She imitated his drawl and made him laugh.

"I don't sound like that." He trapped her gaze, teasing her, exaggerating his accent. "Do I?"

She shook her head and the moment turned gentle, warm and inviting. Too warm, he thought, as his heart stirred. Too inviting.

He blew out a rough breath, breaking the spell. "I told Danforth about our affair."

Her skin paled. "You told my father? Why?"

"I work for him. I wanted him to know the truth."

The ceiling fan whirred, the blades cutting through the air like knives, feathering her hair again. "Are you really interested in being my friend?"

If she were innocent, he thought. If his investigation cleared her name. "Of course I am. In fact, I think we should go out tonight."

"Where?"

"To an art show."

Her eyes lit up. "At the new gallery downtown? I've heard about it."

Michael jammed his hands in his pockets. He didn't want Lea to be the stalker. He didn't want to look into those beautiful eyes and see the vicious things Lady Savannah had done. "My assistant told me about it. Cindy always knows what's going on."

"I don't socialize very much." Distracted, she glanced at a crystal trinket box on the nightstand. "But it took me a while to find a job and get used to this area. I was nervous about moving here, about approaching my father. I've only been in Savannah for eight months." She sighed. "But you must know that already."

Yes, he knew. But he also knew that Lady Savannah had begun to threaten Danforth in February, a month after Lea, his prime suspect, settled in Savannah.

The gallery was located in a three-story historic building, each floor presenting a theme. The garden level was just that, a garden of artistic expression that led to outdoor sculptures and carefully tended foliage.

Lea walked beside Michael, awed by the moment, by the floral fragrance and haunting displays. They stopped in front of a ghostlike statue, a chalk-white female figure with gems in her eyes.

"She looks like she's watching us," Michael said. "But it's just an illusion."

Lea turned to face her companion, wondering if their affair was an illusion. If he would ever return to her bed.

They proceeded to the next sculpture, a male angel with his arms raised to the sky. He was strong and powerful, his armor painted an iridescent shade of blue.

"He's a warring angel." Michael gestured to the slain demons at the celestial being's feet.

"Good versus evil." Lea noticed a row of white flowers circling the display. "Good triumphs."

"So it seems." He tilted his head. "Sometimes it's hard to tell who's good and who's evil."

A lump formed in her throat. Maybe he did suspect her. Maybe he was playing a game of cat and mouse. "Good people are capable of doing bad things."

"Is that a confession?"

"For what?" she asked, testing him, waiting for him to accuse her.

He touched her cheek instead. He looked familiar in the moonlight, her dark-skinned vampire come to life.

"You're so warm," he said.

"The air is warm." She wanted to kiss him, but that would only allow him to taste her anxiety, the fear that he might be investigating her.

"We should go inside." He escorted her to the main entrance on the parlor floor. They took a set of concrete stairs, chipped and faded from wear.

Then suddenly the tone of the gallery changed. Other patrons gathered in the reception area, around a buffet table laden with catered appetizers and multicolored napkins. The lights were bright, the wood floors polished to a high sheen. A cut-glass chandelier cast a glow over a temporary bar, where plastic cups beckoned for tips.

"There's Cindy," Michael said. "My assistant."

Lea watched a tall, stunning blonde approach them. With her strappy heels and trim white suit, she received a slew of admiring glances, turning heads along the way. Her throat was bare, Lea noticed, except for a hint of lace beneath her jacket.

"Michael." The blonde leaned forward to give him a quick peck on the cheek. "You brought a companion."

He introduced the women, and Cindy extended her hand. She was Lea's idea of Savannah chic, with a gilded voice and a blooming smile. Somehow she managed to blend Southern grace with an uptown attitude, a lady who always kept her cell phone charged.

"Well, now." Cindy measured Lea's petite frame and waist-length hair. "Where has my boss been keeping you?"

"In my dungeon," Michael interjected.

"I'll bet. She's beautiful."

Next to Cindy, Lea didn't feel beautiful. She felt small and insignificant in her two-piece silk garment. A *my lai* who'd been pelted with rocks.

"I hope you're both enjoying the show." The blonde clutched a jeweled handbag. On her wrist, she wore a diamond tennis bracelet.

"It's lovely." Lea managed to speak up, wishing she'd chosen an outfit that didn't resemble *Ao Dai*. She tried so hard to be an American, yet here she was, dressed in mock-Vietnamese attire, a long flowing smock and baggy trousers, created by a crafty U.S. designer.

Cindy chatted with Michael, then excused herself, gesturing with her diamond-draped arm. "I'm going to mingle for a while." She turned to Lea. "It was nice meeting you." That said, she departed, leaving Michael and Lea alone.

Silent, they remained near the buffet table, their gazes locked. Cindy's perfume, an orchid mist, still lingered.

"Would you like a drink?" he asked.

"No, thank you." Lea waited a beat. She was curious about Cindy, but she hated to bombard him with questions so quickly. "Are you going to have one?"

"Maybe later."

She thought about the angel in the garden, about good and evil. "How long has Cindy worked for you?"

"About three years."

"Is she your personal assistant?"

"She's my administrative assistant." He smoothed the front of his hair. It was straight and dark, but the auburn highlights had emerged, a reflection from a nearby lamp. "Cindy's very efficient."

"She's stunning."

"Yes, she is." He moved closer. "But she wears too much perfume."

"Is that your only complaint?"

"I'm not a complainer." He moved even closer, his loafers tapping the wood floor. One, two three...and he was there, just inches from her. "I like being around beautiful women."

Lea's heartbeat staggered. She wanted to latch on to his shoulders, to absorb the power of his body, but she wanted to push him away, too. "Have you ever been lovers?"

"Who? Me and Cindy?" His expression turned hard, making his face more angular, his cheekbones more prominent. "That's a hell of a question. But no, we've never been together. She isn't my type."

Liar, she thought. Cindy was nearly every man's type. "Does she have someone in her life?"

"She did. They split up a few months ago. It was his choice. She didn't take it well."

Suddenly Lea felt bad for the other woman. "She loved him?"

Michael shrugged. "I suppose, but she's getting over him now. She has her sights set on someone else."

"Who?"

"I don't know. She hasn't told me his name. But I have a feeling he's a colleague of mine. She's been asking me for advice. Asking me how to get this mystery man to notice her." He laughed at that. "Women can be so dramatic."

"It wouldn't take much to notice her. He must be preoccupied." She glanced around, looking for Cindy, but the blonde had vanished. "I wonder who he is."

"Someone with money, I'll bet. Her last boyfriend was loaded."

Lea recalled the wealthy man she'd dated in Little Saigon, the man who'd destroyed her innocence. "Sometimes rich men use women."

"Cindy's too shrewd to get used."

But I'm not, she thought, as Michael's gaze swept over her. I'm not.

# Three

Michael and Lea wandered around the gallery and Lea stopped at an unusual display.

"This is my favorite artist." She moved closer to the three-dimensional wall hanging, a larger-than-life piece comprised of discarded objects. "They say he turns trash into treasure. He finds things in junkyards and Dumpsters and makes something important out of them."

Michael didn't respond. He just looked at Lea, at her long, flowing hair and delicate profile. He wanted to tell her that she wasn't an unwanted object. That she was strong and beautiful.

But then he thought about Lady Savannah and the tenderness in his heart twisted like vines, leaving him in a state of confusion.

Stalking was a serious crime, a dangerous crime. Michael had spent countless hours holed up in his office, poring over Danforth's case, trying to piece together the puzzle. And the clues kept leading to Lea.

To the woman he wanted to hold at night.

"I'm ready for that drink," he said, anxious to dull his senses. "What about you?"

"No, thank you. I'd like to stay here."

With the trash that had been turned into treasure, he thought. With old rakes and paintbrushes and books with torn covers. With greeting cards not good enough to save, with letters someone had thrown away.

"Why don't I bring you a drink?" he said. She couldn't seem to take her eyes off the display and he imagined her disappearing into it, slipping into scenery that made her feel safe.

"Maybe some cranberry juice." She remained where she was, her gaze fixed on the wall hanging. "With a little ice."

He went downstairs, wondering if he should have offered her a plate of food, too. The parlor floor was still busy, still bustling with art patrons enjoying the festivities.

He ordered a beer for himself and juice for Lea. He spotted Cindy with a group of Savannah socialites, but luckily she didn't see him. He didn't want her accompanying him upstairs and intruding on Lea's solitude. It didn't take a genius to figure out that Cindy intimidated Lea, that the dark-haired beauty didn't feel comfortable around the statuesque blonde.

He returned to Lea, only to find her in the same

frame of mind, lost in a world of throwaway art. He handed her the cranberry juice.

"Thank you."

"You're welcome." He had the notion to run his hand along her cheek, but his fingers were cold from carrying the drinks.

Did she know how much alike they were? he wondered. That somewhere deep down, they were connected?

"How do you say half-breed in your language?" he asked.

Her skin paled. "Why?"

"Because I want to know."

She didn't answer.

"Tell me, Lea. Tell me what it is."

She took a step back, moving away from him, making him feel like a monster. He couldn't imagine how he was going to feel if she were guilty, if he had to turn her over to the authorities.

"Just say it," he persisted, pushing her for a response.

*"Con lai,"* she snapped.

"Did people call you that?"

"Yes." Her pretty features distorted, signifying her pain.

Michael reached out to skim her cheek, giving in to the need to touch her. "People used to call me a half-breed when I was growing up."

"Because you're part American Indian?"

He nodded and took his hand away, knowing he'd left her chilled. His hands were still cold. "Even my dad called me that. He was white. My mother was from the Seminole Nation."

Her voice quavered. "Your father was cruel to you?"

"Not with his fists, but with his words." He glanced at the artwork consuming the gallery wall. "Every time he put me down, I was determined to make something of myself. To prove that I was better than him."

"And what about your mother? What kind of relationship did you have with her?"

"It was strained. She was obsessed with my dad, with the affairs he was having. Whenever she suspected him of cheating, she went ballistic, clawing and scratching at him, screaming so everyone in the neighborhood knew what was going on."

"He had no right to cheat on her." Lea clutched her cup, holding it to her chest. "She was his wife. She deserved better."

"I know. But the way she carried on just made things worse. Sometimes she used to throw his clothes onto the lawn, right in front of our apartment building." Michael could still recall the shame, the embarrassment that overwhelmed him. "People thought she was crazy. That screwy Seminole, they used to say. That schizoid squaw." He paused, took a breath. "I hated people calling her that."

"Schizoid?"

"Squaw."

"Is that a dirty word?"

"Some say it translates to the totality of being female, which is a good thing. But others think it's slanderous and offensive. That it refers to a woman's private parts."

"Your neighbors didn't mean it in a good way when they said it about your mother."

"No, they didn't." He turned, looking for an escape route. "I need some air. Do you want to join me?"

She nodded and they proceeded outside, where a third-story balcony overlooked a collection of historic buildings.

The summer air proved muggy, but Michael was grateful for the Southern sky. He leaned against the wrought-iron rail and drank his beer.

Lea stood beside him. She'd barely touched her drink, the ice in her cup melting into the bloodred liquid, thinning the contents.

"My dad had a thing for blondes," he said. "I have no idea why he married a Seminole."

"He cheated with women like Cindy?"

"I never said anything about Cindy. You can't lump all blondes together."

Her chin shot up. "I wasn't."

"Weren't you?" he accused. "Cindy isn't a bad person. She's just tough. She grew up the way I did. Poor, determined to climb her way to the top."

"She doesn't seem sincere."

"Do I?" he asked.

Lea didn't respond. She sipped her watered-down juice instead.

"I don't, do I?" Because he wasn't, he thought. Because he suspected her of a crime. "I like you, Lea. I swear, that's the truth. I feel something for you."

Her eyes locked onto his. "Something?"

He set his cup on a nearby ledge. "Kinship. Lust. Confusion. I'm not sure if I can explain what I feel."

"You just did." She gave him a shaky smile. "I feel those things, too."

"Why haven't we ever talked before now?" He dragged his hand through his hair. "We slept together for a month and we barely communicated. I've never been that callous with a woman before."

"Are you apologizing to me, Michael?"

"Yes." God help him, he was. But that wouldn't stop him from investigating her.

"I'm not very good at relationships." She tilted her head and moonlight framed her face, casting a silvery glow over her skin. "There was a man in California, in Little Saigon. I thought I loved him. I thought he loved me."

"What happened?"

"I slept with him." She sipped her drink, the ice still melting. "I wanted to wait until we were married, but he said I didn't need to remain a virgin."

Michael studied her posture, the tension in her shoulders. "He took advantage of you."

"I was young. Only nineteen. He was older than me, close to thirty. A wealthy Vietnamese businessman, very traditional. I should have known better. He had no intention of marrying me. It didn't matter if we were in America. I was still *con lai* to him." She set her cup next to Michael's. "He bought me pretty things, but I didn't know I was his whore. Not until he told me he was marrying someone else, a girl his family approved of."

"And what did you do, Lea?"

"I worked hard to better myself, to get a college education, to stop being *con lai*."

"There's nothing wrong with being a half-breed. It's who we are. It makes us special."

"It doesn't make me feel special."

"I know. I've been fighting that feeling all my life." He looked into her eyes and saw a reflection of himself. "Are you ashamed of your mother's culture? Of the things she taught you?"

"Sometimes. But I don't want to be."

"Then share some of it with me."

"How?" She seemed lost, like the child she'd once been, a little girl who'd never found her place in society.

"You can teach me how to make a Vietnamese meal. Tomorrow, after we both get home from work."

"It's been so long since I've—"

He placed his finger over her lips. "Don't make excuses. Just say yes."

When he took his hand away, she didn't say yes. But she didn't say no, either. She simply watched him, and he wondered what she was thinking.

"Are you going to share your mother's culture with me?" she asked.

Michael realized he didn't have a choice. He couldn't expect something from her that he wasn't willing to give. "I'll do the best I can."

She assessed his response. "The best you can?"

"There are a lot of things I was never taught. My mother gave up her traditions to marry my father, to live his way." He reached for his beer and finished it, combating the dryness in his throat. "Her family was from the Big Cypress Reservation in Florida, but she moved to Atlanta to be with my dad. That's where I was raised."

"I thought you were from Savannah."

"No. I moved here later. After I got out of the service, after my mother died."

"Is your father gone, too?"

He shrugged. "I have no idea. He split when I was still in high school. He left my mom and me with nothing." Nothing but a roach-infested apartment and a welfare check, he thought. "She cried for him almost every night. She waited for him to come back."

Lea moved closer. "Why did she love him so much?"

"It wasn't love. Not in a healthy sense of the word." Michael glanced up the sky, at the stars lighting up the night. "She was fixated on him, on everything he did, and he knew how to charm her, especially after an argument."

"But he didn't charm you."

"I'm not a woman. He had a way with women."

Her voice turned soft. "So do you."

"Not like him." Michael had the urge to kiss her, to drag her against his body and release the tightness in his chest, the ache of needing her. But he wasn't about to play his father's game.

He was already guilty of keeping the spark between them alive, of inviting her to his home, of toying with both of their emotions in a dark and dangerous way.

The following evening, after Lea's workday ended, she arrived at Michael's house using the security code he'd given her to open the electronic gate. With her arms full of groceries, she tackled the keyless-entry front door and headed straight for the kitchen. After placing the bags on the counter, she spotted a hand-written note from Michael.

*Don't start the meal without me.*

Fine, she thought. But where was he? And how long would he be gone?

Unsure of what else to do, she unpacked the groceries and then went upstairs to change, to remove her summer suit, panty hose and heels. Lea worked for CCS Enterprises, a networking and consulting firm that specialized in corporate computer solutions, and her position required professional attire.

Eager to relax, she slipped on a pair of jeans and a T-shirt, then banded her hair into a ponytail. But by the time she descended the stairs, she got an ominous feeling.

A feeling that she was being watched.

Did Michael have surveillance cameras hidden throughout his home? Had he left her alone purposely? Was she being filmed?

She looked around the great room, telling herself to quit being so paranoid. Of course Michael had surveillance cameras in his home, but he probably only used them when he was protecting a client, when he and his security team were inspecting the premises for intruders.

He wouldn't film a lover.

Would he?

The front door opened, and she froze, like a proverbial deer caught in the headlights.

"Evening." Michael filled the doorway, with his broad shoulders and tall, muscular frame. He wore a black suit, a white shirt and a gray-and-black tie. His hair caught a ray of the setting sun and his jacket was slung over his arm.

"Hi." She managed a casual greeting, even if her heart was pounding at warp speed. After a moment of awkward silence, her anxiety returned. "Where were you?"

He closed the door. "At the office."

"But you left me a note."

"I wrote that this morning, before I went to work. You were already gone and I didn't get a chance to talk to you."

"I had an early meeting." She dusted some imaginary lint from her T-shirt. "Are you hungry?"

"You bet. I need to change, then we can get started on the meal."

He headed toward the staircase, but she stopped him. "I thought you were working a light schedule."

"I am. This is light for me. I'm not usually home for dinner." He loosened his tie. "Do I have time for a shower?"

Lea's mouth went dry. How was she supposed to stay here for the next two weeks, missing him, wishing they were still lovers?

"Of course you have time for a shower." She proceeded to the kitchen to get a glass of water, to focus on the food, to keep her mind occupied.

He returned fifteen minutes later, wearing drawstring sweatpants and a tank top. When he moved closer to inspect the ingredients on the counter, she noticed the ends of his hair were damp and he smelled like her favorite soap.

"So what are we making?" he asked.

"Chicken with lemongrass and a rice-noodle salad." Recipes she'd chosen just for him. "They're both fairly simple to make."

"Good." He sent her a boyish grin. "You know I'm not a very creative cook." He picked up a glass bottle. "What's this?"

"*Nuoc mam.* Fish sauce. It's used as a condiment and a flavoring. The way soy sauce is used in Chinese cooking." She took the chicken out of the refrigerator. "I found the *nuoc mam* at an international market. I bought chopsticks, too."

"Really?" He gave her another heart-stirring grin. "I'm glad you agreed to do this."

"So am I." Lea tried to think of something else to say, but she couldn't seem to find her voice. She hadn't expected Michael's interest in her culture to make her want him even more. Still silent, she unwrapped the chopsticks.

"What are you thinking about?" he asked.

You, she wanted to say. The nights they used to make love, the sensation of his mouth against her skin, the bedroom murmurs he'd whispered in her ear.

She glanced down, avoiding his gaze. "I'm thinking about the chopsticks."

"What about them?"

"They became a popular eating utensil because they could replace knives at the dinner table."

"And why was that important?"

She looked up, meeting the curiosity in his eyes, the electricity between them. "Knives were associated with war and death, but chopsticks were used in pairs, so they represented harmony, prospect and peace."

"That's nice. Really nice." He reached out to smooth a strand of her hair away from her face. Already pieces were coming loose from her ponytail. "You're going to have to show me the proper way to use them."

"I will." She just stood there, letting him touch her, letting him make her weak-kneed and girlish. Submissive. "I feel like *Miss Saigon.*" A feeling that troubled her.

He stepped back. "What do you mean?"

"Nothing." Uncomfortable, she cut the chicken into small pieces, keeping her hands busy. "You can chop the cabbage for the salad."

They worked side by side, with Lea instructing him from time to time. While she fried garlic and onions, he leaned against the counter, watching her.

"Tell me about the man you dated in California."

She sprinkled ground chilies and minced lemongrass into the pan. "I already told you about him."

"What was his name?"

"Thao."

"I'm sorry he hurt you."

"I was naive." She added the chicken, stirring it with a wooden spoon. "I thought living in America would make a difference. But Thao was too traditional to want a wife like me."

Michael boiled the noodles for the salad. "Did you date anyone in Vietnam?"

"No. Never."

"There weren't any Amerasian boys who asked you out?"

She shook her head. "I was the only *my lai* in the village where I lived. Besides, couples in Vietnam don't date the way they do in America. A boy must introduce himself to a girl's family and seek their approval before he can take her out. And even then, it's very proper. They don't kiss or touch or hold hands in public."

"Are girls supposed to remain virgins until they get married?"

"Yes. But it doesn't matter that I slept with Thao. It was a long time ago, and I can't keep dwelling on the past."

"You're an incredible lover, Lea."

She nearly dropped the spoon. She could feel Michael's body heat, feel his gaze sweeping over her. "Thao was my only lover. Besides you."

"Then I'm honored." He touched her hair again, tucking a strand behind her ear. "But it isn't right for us to sleep together anymore."

"Why?" she asked, her voice barely audible, her pulse leaping to her throat.

"Because I don't want to use you."

She found the courage to question him further, to say what she was thinking. "What if I decide to use you?"

He raised his brows at her, shifted his feet, frowned and then ended up with a half-cocked smile on his face. "Do I look like a helpless male to you? A guy who could get used?"

"No. But men like sex." She lifted her chin. "You like sex. And that gives me power."

"Spoken like a true woman." He came up behind her, bringing her closer to the stove, crowding her, making her much too aware of him. "Don't burn the chicken."

"I'm not." Flustered, she pushed him back, nudging his chest with her shoulder. He'd taken the power away from her. He'd made her weak-kneed again.

And Lea tried so hard to be strong, to fight the chains, the emotional turmoil, that bound her.

# Four

Michael and Lea decided to eat on the patio, at a glass-topped table, decorated with citronella candles. The dancing flames and fragrant smoke presented a compelling atmosphere. And so did a distant view of the marsh.

It almost seemed like a date. Almost, Michael thought. But not quite. His relationship with Lea grew more complicated by the minute. He missed their affair, the midnight rendezvous and secret passion.

"It's beautiful here." She sipped her tea. "I like being outside."

"Me, too." He studied the teapot and the tiny cups she'd purchased at the international market. They looked so domestic, so feminine. Just like her.

No wonder she turned him on. Lea was everything

he'd always wanted, everything he used to hope for. She was strong yet gentle. Understated yet elegant. When he climbed into bed at night, he longed to feel her body next to his.

"Sometimes I wonder if I'm fooling myself," he said.

"About what?"

"The white-picket-fence thing. A wife, kids, a friendly pooch in the yard."

"Why? Because your life is more of an electronic-gate, guard-dog-type thing?"

"Exactly." His career took precedence over everything, especially the relationships in his life. "You're an observant lady, Lea."

"I try."

No, he thought. She did more than try. She made decisions with her heart and analyzed them with her head. And she was too smart not to worry about her situation, to not wonder if he considered her a suspect.

He adjusted his chopsticks, handling them fairly well for a beginner. But Michael did everything fairly well. He took pride in being competent. "Tell me about your job."

"What's to tell? You already know what I do. You have a file on me."

"That isn't the same as hearing you talk about yourself. I want to get to know the real you." The woman who might be Lady Savannah, he thought.

She tasted her chicken, utilizing her chopsticks as easily as she wielded a fork. "I'm a computer systems analyst. I improve existing computer systems, as well as develop new systems."

"So you write programs?"

"Sometimes. CSS, the company I work for, specializes in corporate solutions. We tailor computer systems to fit our customers' needs."

"What about viruses?"

She stopped breathing. "What about them?"

"I was just wondering if you've had any significant experience in that realm. If you've ever designed security software."

"No, I haven't. But isn't my job history tucked away in that file?" She blew out the breath she'd been holding. "I don't understand why you're asking me about things you already know."

He sat back in his chair, luring her into his trap, loving his job, hating it, wishing he didn't have feelings for her. "You're getting defensive."

She reached for her tea, cradling the cup, grasping the tiny blue flowers painted on the porcelain. "That file bothers me."

He remained where he was, his posture easy, his mind sharp. "As it should. I wouldn't want someone investigating me just because I was a politician's illegitimate daughter."

"You're not anyone's daughter, Michael. You're a man." That said, she resumed eating, putting him in his place.

Just as she lifted a glob of rice to her mouth, he came forward in his chair. "I think you should help me with my case."

The rice nearly fell onto her plate. "What case?"

"The one I'm working on for your dad. I could really use a woman's perspective."

"I'm not a detective."

"But you harbor resentment toward your father. And so does the suspect in my case. You might be able to help me figure her out."

She jammed the rice into her mouth, but she didn't go after another bite. The chopsticks landed on the table, untouched. So much for harmony, prospect and peace, he thought.

"Figure whom out?" she finally asked. "Who is she?"

"A woman who's been stalking your dad."

She froze. She literally didn't move, and he realized his words had stunned her. If she were Lady Savannah, she hadn't thought of herself as "a stalker." But most stalkers didn't. They justified their behavior on their own terms.

"We can get into the specifics later," he said. "When we have time to go over my notes. Maybe Saturday."

"That's five days away."

"There's no hurry." He wanted her to fret about it, to wake up every morning and wonder what he had up his sleeve.

"I'd rather discuss it now."

"I'd prefer to wait. I don't want to spoil this beautiful evening talking about another woman." He scooped up some of the salad, looked directly in her eyes. "Not while I'm dining with you."

Lea turned on the bedside lamp, flooding her room with light. She couldn't sleep; all she could think about was the case Michael had mentioned.

Was he being sincere in asking for her help? Or was this his way of trapping her?

Much too warm, she pushed away the covers. After she went into the bathroom to rinse her face, to wash away the anxiety, shame coiled in her belly like a snake.

He'd called her a stalker. For some naive reason, Lea had never associated that word with the things she'd done. But apparently that was what Michael had termed Lady Savannah. That was her criminal calling card.

She leaned against the sink, holding her stomach, trying to keep the snake from striking, even though she knew she deserved to get bitten.

When her mouth turned dry, she crept downstairs for a glass of ice water, for something to temper the discomfort.

An amber night-light cast a ghostly glow in the kitchen, creating odd-shaped shadows on the walls. On silent feet, she opened a cabinet, grateful the hinges didn't creak. As she placed her glass beneath the ice dispenser, the frozen cubes made a crashing sound, jarring the stillness, making her heart jump out of her chest.

Feeling foolish, she added the water and took a sip, cooling her fears, quenching her thirst. And then Michael's voice came out of nowhere.

"Are you all right?"

She spun around to see him standing in the doorway, wearing a pair of loose-fitting shorts and little else. His chest was bare and his straight dark hair was tousled, falling across his forehead rebelliously.

She glanced at his stomach and noticed how low his shorts rode on his hips. What would he do if she seduced him? If she whispered something erotic in his ear? Lea wanted to make love with him again, to pretend their relationship was real. "I'm fine."

"You don't look fine. You look pale."

"Do I?" He looked like a bronzed statue, strong and solid, with chiseled features. He moved closer and she wondered if his skin was cool to the touch. "I couldn't sleep. I was hot."

"I can turn up the air conditioner."

"That's okay. There's a fan above my bed."

"You just said you were hot."

"I am. I was." She sipped her water again. "I'm better now."

He came over to her, pressing his hand against her forehead. Her bones almost melted, and she cursed his proximity.

"You don't feel feverish."

"Because I'm not. I told you I'm fine."

He trapped her gaze. "Do you ever sleep?"

His eyes were magnetic, his irises flecked with light. Suddenly she feared he would hypnotize her, trick her into admitting her crimes.

"Do you?" she asked.

"Do I what?"

"Ever sleep?"

"Not much. Not lately." He dropped his hand and stepped back. "What did you mean earlier when you said you felt like *Miss Saigon?*"

Her pulse pounded at her neck. "I didn't mean anything."

"You wouldn't have said it if meant nothing."

"*Miss Saigon* is a play," she told him.

"I know. I've heard of it." He shifted his weight. "What's it about?"

"The heroine has an affair with an American soldier. And after he leaves, she gives birth to his son." She paused. "A child like me."

Michael frowned, and Lea feared she might be falling in love with him. That somewhere deep down, she was losing her soul. Why else would she want to sleep him with him again? Crave to be in his arms?

"That sounds more like Lan's story than yours," he said.

She nodded, her emotions too close to the surface. "My mother waited for my father to come back for her. To bring us to America." Tears burned her eyes, but she wouldn't let them fall. "She always said good things about him. She believed in his honor."

"Then maybe you should, too."

"I did when I was a little girl. I waited right along with my mother, thinking he would save us from our persecution." The glass began sweating in her hand. "But he was here, in Savannah, with his wife and other children."

"He needs you to forgive him."

And what about what I need? she thought. What about her feelings for Michael? "I don't want to discuss my father with you. Not now."

He sighed, and they both turned quiet. Shadows still haunted the walls and the microwave clock displayed an after-midnight hour.

"I still don't understand why you felt like *Miss Saigon*," he said, breaking the silence.

"Sometimes you make me weak," she admitted. "Submissive. Not like an American girl."

"You think American women don't stumble into affairs? Don't get mixed up with the wrong men?"

Her chest constricted. "Are you the wrong man?"

"You know damn well I am."

"Because you're my father's bodyguard?"

"Yes," he said solemnly.

"Then why did you keep coming back to my apartment? Why didn't you just leave it as a one-night stand?"

He thrust his hand through his hair, pushing the errant strands away from his forehead. "I couldn't stay away. I wanted you too much."

"But you don't want me now?" she challenged.

His gaze roamed over her, and she realized how she must look, her nightgown clinging to her body, floating around her ankles like mist.

"I don't want to use you, Lea. I already told you that."

"And I already told you that I should have the right to use you." She set her glass on the counter and then turned to face him again, letting him see the woman she was. "Why should you call all the shots? Why should you make all the decisions?"

"You want to talk about decisions?" He cursed and grabbed her wrist, slamming her palm against his chest, forcing her to hit him. "About calling the shots?"

Lea tried to pull way, but he kept her there, his heart pounding wildly beneath her fingers. "Michael—"

"This is what you do to me. This is my weakness." His heart thumped even harder. So hard, he fought his next breath. "Do you think it's easy for me to give you up? To keep my hands off you?" He cursed again, a crude word, a sexual word, the act he wanted to commit. "I'm going crazy."

Lea pulled free of his grasp. "Now you know how I felt, waiting for you night after night. Wondering how long our affair would last."

"I was wrong. Damn it. I was wrong. But getting too close to you scared me."

And now they were arguing, she thought. Battling their feelings for each other. "Go back to bed, Michael."

"What for? I won't be able to sleep."

Neither would she, but what else were they supposed to do?

He reached out to graze her cheek, to touch her as gently as he could, but Lea backed away, her heart lodged in her throat, her emotions spinning out of control.

Getting close to him scared her, too. Yet she needed him, more than she'd ever needed anyone.

Michael awakened in a fog and glanced at the window, trying to make sense of his drifting-on-a-dream state. It was still dark out; the sheers were shrouded in moonlight.

He rolled over, his eyelids heavy. But a moment later, a creaking sound caught his attention and he shifted his gaze to the door, where the night-darkened image of a woman stood.

He blinked, certain he must have conjured her up in his mind. That she was an illusion. That his eyes and his ears were playing tricks on him.

The illusion moved forward, just a little, like a fragment in time, an all-too-real dream.

No, not a dream. He was awake. "Lea?"

"Yes." She responded to him, her voice as smoky as her image.

He didn't turn on the lamp, afraid she would disappear with the light, afraid he would lose her for good. "Why are you here?"

"To touch you. To take what I need."

Heat flooded his body, like wax melting over his skin, seeping into his pores.

She stepped farther into the room and he knew he should send her away, stop her from seducing him. But he was already aroused, already ignoring the danger of getting caught in her web.

Deep down, he knew she was Lady Savannah. With each day that passed, the clues got stronger, the truth hovering in the air. But tonight he didn't care. Tonight he wanted her.

He waited, watching. She paused at the foot of the bed and slipped off her nightgown. He squinted to see her clearer, to force his eyes to adjust, to combat the darkness.

She was wearing panties; that much he could tell. He could see them, an iridescent swatch of cotton between her legs. When she removed them, anticipation pounded at every pulse point in his body, making him ache.

"You shouldn't be doing this," he said.

She crawled onto the bed and leaned over him, her unbound hair falling like silk, her lotion-scented skin grazing his. "This is my power, Michael. It's the only advantage I have over you."

He thought about the commitment he'd made to find Lady Savannah, to bring her to justice. "I can't make any promises. I can't give you a future."

"I'm not asking you to." She rubbed her mouth across his. "I'm doing this for me."

She kissed him, soft and slow and sweet. She was naked, clinging to his shoulders, making his heart skip erratic beats. She moved down his body, and he sensed her purpose, the erotic act she intended to perform.

She licked his navel, tracing a path with her tongue, tugging at his shorts, removing them. Michael lifted his hips, eager to surrender, to give her everything she'd come to take.

Everything and more.

He threaded his hands through her hair and the dark mass caressed his thighs. The ultimate seduction, he thought. It thrilled him, shamed him, made him curse the ache between his legs. And then she touched him there, a featherlight kiss, a promise of pleasure.

Michael thought he might die.

"You're so warm. So hard." She wrapped her hand around him, preparing for her next move.

"I want to turn on the light. I want to watch." He reached for the lamp, and she took him into her mouth, barely giving him time to think, to react, to do anything but pray for relief. A golden light flooded her image, giving him a dream-enhanced view.

He opened his legs, accommodating her, allowing her to set a smooth, sensual rhythm. He moved with her, making love to her mouth, caressing her face, losing part of his soul.

"Lea." He said her name and she looked up at him. Their eyes met and held, creating even more intimacy.

She took him deeper, so deep he hit the back of her throat. He shivered, wondering if he'd ever been this aroused, this desperate for a woman.

Before it ended, before he lost control, he pulled her up and ran his hands all over her body, making her sigh.

"Let me do it to you," he said.

She smoothed a strand of his hair. "You used to do it all the time."

"That's right, I did." He skimmed her cheek. "And I know just how you like it."

She smiled, and he kissed her. Tonight they would do everything, he thought. Every erotic thing they could think of, every position that gave them pleasure.

Anxious, he lifted her legs onto his shoulders, and she arched against his mouth.

She was warm and wet, sweet and musky. He filled himself with her flavor, teasing her with his tongue, arousing her the way she'd aroused him.

She touched herself, heightening the sensation, the need to be naughty, to make the feeling last. He licked between her fingers, and she made throaty little sounds.

As she fisted his hair, he looked up at her. Everything about her turned him on: the shape of her eyes, the color of her skin, the subtle curve of her hips. She rocked against his mouth, urging him to kiss her in that special place, to make her come.

And when it happened, he tasted her release, the pleasure convulsing her body.

Beautiful, dangerous Lea. He should have resisted

her, but her magic was too strong. Michael lifted his head, and she smiled at him, drugged from her orgasm.

"I don't want tonight to end," she said.

"It's not over yet." He reached into the nightstand drawer and fished around for a condom, securing the foil packet.

They caressed each other, rolling over the bed, tangling the sheets. Her hair fanned across the pillow and over her breasts, making her look even more exotic. He loved her hair, the long flowing length, the silky texture.

Sensation slid over sensation, the rhythm sleek and inviting. He rode her; she climbed on top of him; he straddled her. They kept switching places, driving each other half mad.

He withdrew, then entered her again, intensifying the feeling. Their gazes locked and their fingers entwined, completing the symmetry. They were good together, he thought. So damn good. Yet he knew it was wrong.

She wrapped her legs around him, holding him close, dragging his mouth to hers, kissing him. And then she climaxed in his arms, all warm and soft and beautiful.

Michael closed his eyes and let himself fall, spilling into her, lost in the feeling of being her lover.

# Five

**D**awn streamed through the window sheers, awakening Lea in a morning-after haze. She rolled over and landed against warm, solid flesh.

Michael.

She'd stayed in his room; she'd slept in his bed. Rising onto her elbows, she leaned over him, peering down at his face.

His eyes were closed, his hair mussed, his jaw peppered with beard stubble. He looked gloriously rumpled, a man who'd made hot, hard-driving love last night.

Lea glanced lower, at his chest and stomach. The sheet was draped low on his hips, exposing the shadow of hair that led to his—

"What are you looking at?"

She jumped back. "I thought you were asleep."

"You were checking out my—"

"I was not." Her cheeks flamed. She could feel them turning a thousand shades of pink. He was half-aroused. She could see the masculine shape through the sheet, tenting the fabric between his legs.

He mocked her with his brows, raising them in smart-aleck amusement, and she realized she was naked too, completely exposed to his high-and-mighty gaze. Self-conscious, she searched around for her nightgown and found it at the foot of the bed, along with her discarded panties.

"You're not so brave in the daylight," he said.

She put on her clothes, then reached for her pillow and smacked him with it. She hated the way he made her feel. The nervousness he never failed to evoke.

Stunned, he merely stared at her. "What the hell was that for?"

"You're supposed to cuddle with me, not complain about being seduced."

"You want to cuddle?" He lunged, grabbed her, pinned her to the bed. And then he tickled her, his hands rough yet gentle. Big and strong and boyish.

She laughed; she squirmed; she melted like a pat of honey-flavored butter. She'd never interacted this way with anyone before. Her life had been filled with serious issues.

"You have no shame." She tried to swat his bare butt, but he kept eluding her. "You're getting turned on by this."

He secured her wrists, holding them above her head. "I knew you were looking down there."

"I can feel it, Michael."

"'Cause it's so big."

She bit her lip to keep from laughing. He was poking her stomach, trying to make his overinflated, male ego point. "It's not that big."

"Says the woman who can't wait to touch it again."

"That's not what I meant by cuddling." She broke free, and they grinned like a couple of foolhardy kids. But when he moved a strand of hair away from her cheek, tucking it gently behind her ear, they stopped smiling and gazed at each other, silent in the morning light.

"We shouldn't be getting this close," he said.

"I know." But how was she supposed to stop herself from falling in love with him? How was she supposed to pretend it wasn't happening? "I'll only be here for two weeks. We're not talking about an eternity."

He was still poised above her, his naked body brushing her nightgown, leaving shivers along her skin.

"I wish it could be different, Lea."

"Me, too." But deep down she knew he was suspicious of her. He hadn't come right out and accused her of stalking Abraham Danforth, but she could see it in his eyes, drifting between them like a bad dream.

She skimmed his jaw, wishing she wasn't the woman he was investigating, the lady who'd plotted her childhood revenge, who'd destroyed the only chance she'd ever had at happiness.

"Do you want to get ready in here?" he asked.

She nodded. She had to get dressed for work and so, she assumed, did he. "I need to get my toiletries first."

"That's fine." He waited for her in the master bathroom, the place designed for a married couple, with his and her sinks.

When she returned, he was in the process of shaving. She went about her daily routine, as well.

After she removed her nightgown in front of a mirrored wall beside the tub, he came up behind her, slipping his arms around her waist.

"Do you want to take a bath with me?" she asked.

"Not yet." He slid his hand down the front of her panties, rubbing her, making her wet.

"Michael." She whispered his name, the sound soft and sensual, even to her own ears.

He met her gaze in the mirror, and she knew he wanted her to watch. So she did. She watched everything he did.

After he pushed her panties halfway down her legs, he thumbed her nipples, leaving her warm and wanton. Lea took a deep breath, letting him seduce her, letting him make her heart beat much too fast.

"Lean forward," he said.

She pressed her hands against the glass, her heart pounding even harder. "Like this?"

"Yes." He rubbed the front of his body against the back of hers, sending a trail of heat along her spine.

He was going to make love to her in this position, she thought. He was already hard, already nuzzling her neck.

When he showed her the condom in his hand, she

marveled at how effortlessly he'd acquired the foil packet from a bathroom drawer. "Do you keep those everywhere?"

"A guy needs to be prepared." He sheathed himself, then angled her hips to accept his penetration.

He entered her slowly, sensuously, intensifying the moment. Lea focused on the mirror, not wanting to miss their naked reflections, the image of their joining.

He kept moving inside her, taking what he wanted. The motion was warm and compelling, a rhythm that flowed through her veins, making her dizzy. She could feel him thrusting deeper, stroking her womb.

She twisted her head to kiss him, to slip her tongue into his mouth. He tasted like spearmint, like the flavor of spring. She inhaled his aftershave, an icy-blue sensation filling her senses.

He pressed against her, pushing her forward, flattening her breasts against the mirror. The glass was smooth and cool, but her nipples were hard, stimulated from the pressure.

"Lea." He bit the back of her neck, like a stallion, a feral animal on the verge of climaxing.

She closed her eyes and let it happen to her, the rough, carnal feeling sweeping her away.

A few hours later, Michael sat across from Clayton Crawford in the other man's office. Clay owned Steam, a trendy club and restaurant downtown. Michael had provided the initial security for Steam, and within no time, their association had developed into a strong and loyal friendship. They were both Indian mixed bloods who'd battled their way to success. Clay had grown up poor, too. Not poverty-stricken like Michael, but poor enough to be considered from the wrong side of the tracks.

"So you think she's the stalker," Clay said, pondering their conversation.

Michael nodded. He'd confided in his friend about Lea. At this point, he needed to talk to someone and Clay was the logical choice. Michael wasn't ready to go to Danforth to spill his suspicions.

"And you're sleeping with her?" the other man asked.

"Best damn sex I've ever had."

That got a smile out of Clay. "Then screw the stalking thing. Who the hell cares?"

They looked at each other and laughed. There was no way Michael could ignore the stalking issue, but Clay's twisted humor helped him relax. "I feel like such a bastard. Like I'm using her."

"Reality check, buddy. She came to your room last night."

"And I kept going to her apartment before that."

"You didn't suspect her then."

"Well, I do now."

Clay picked up a paperweight from his desk. The glass object was shaped like a dolphin, reminding Michael of Danforth's seaside mansion. "Her father is going to be furious."

"That you're banging her?"

"That she's the one who threatened him. He already knows we're sleeping together." He gave Clay a harsh look. "And I'm not *banging* her. It's more than that."

The club owner raised his brows. "Good God, Mike, listen to yourself. You're falling for her. You're getting emotionally attached."

"And you're less than three weeks away from the altar." He shifted uncomfortably in his chair. "I don't see where that gives you room to talk."

"I'm not in love with a stalker."

"Did I say I was in love? It's just an affair."

"But not a banging-her-type affair." Clay put down the paperweight. "Makes me wonder what kind of affair it is."

"One that's driving me nuts."

"So what are you going to do?"

"I don't know." He finished his coffee, pushing the cup away. He'd already juiced his veins with caffeine earlier. Pretty soon he'd be bouncing off the walls. "Got any suggestions?"

Clay leaned back, looking like the lord of the hotspot manor. His club reigned over Savannah society, giving him the respect he'd always craved.

"Well?" Michael said, prodding him for a response.

"Do you think she feels bad about what she did?" his friend asked.

"I don't know. I hope so."

"Maybe you should bank on that for a while."

"You mean try to guilt-trip her into a confession? I already asked her to help me with the investigation."

"Then keep going in that direction. Immerse her in the stalking thing."

"And wait for her to come clean?" Michael blew a rough breath. "It's a dangerous game."

"Yes, it is. But at least you're giving her a chance."

Michael nodded, and Clay drummed his fingers on his desk. The window in his office sent a stream of light across his face. His features were hard and angular, reflecting his heritage. Michael supposed he bore a similar look. "Lea had a difficult life. In her country, she was a half-breed, like us."

"Technically I'm a quarter-breed, and having a difficult life is no excuse for what she did."

"I know. And that's the part that's twisting my gut. How am I supposed to forgive her? Hell, I don't even know if I'm part of her scheme, if she's playing me for a fool. Her vulnerability could be a ruse."

"Great sex messes with a guy's brain."

"That it does." Yet he couldn't wait to make love with Lea again, to taste all that warm scented skin, to kiss her, to hold her. "I could get addicted to being with her."

Clay frowned. "I think you already are."

"Maybe she isn't the stalker. Maybe—"

"Maybe what?"

"Nothing. I know she's Lady Savannah." He cursed his hunger for her, the obsession weaving its way into his bloodstream. "I can feel it."

"Yeah, but you don't have enough evidence to rat on her."

"Rat on her? It's my job. It's what I do."

"Sorry. Poor choice of words."

Michael shrugged. "I'm already bending the law. I shouldn't be sleeping with her."

"You're a private investigator. It's not as risky for you to bend the law, not like a cop. But when push comes to shove, you'll do the right thing."

"I'll turn her in," Michael said.

"Yes," Clay agreed. "You will."

At noon, Michael decided to stop by Lea's job, to pay her an unexpected visit.

CSS Enterprises was located in the financial district, with offices that consisted of gray cubicles and an array of employees, each assigned to his or her mousetrap-type space. Michael had always pitied people who worked in crowded, colorless environments, probably because it reminded him of being poor—an unimportant speck on the wall of society. Of course, Lea made a fairly decent wage, with medical benefits stirred into the mix. CSS wasn't a sweatshop.

He asked for directions to her cubicle and found her hunched over her keyboard, typing at a rapid speed. She didn't notice him, so he took a moment to study her.

She wore a lavender-colored blouse and a matching skirt, but he'd seen her get dressed this morning. He shifted his stance, recalling what she had going on under her clothes. Her front-closure bra was beige and her panties were the thong variety, with a hint of ladylike lace.

She glanced up and saw him. "Michael? What are you doing here?"

He stepped into her cubicle. "I was thinking about your underwear."

"What?" She looked around for eavesdroppers. "Is this a joke?"

"No. I came by to ask if you could get away for lunch, but then I started thinking about your panties and bra."

Lea dragged him farther into the confined space, offering him a chair that was crammed against a makeshift wall. He sat, tempted to pull her onto his lap, to shock the nerdiness out of her computer-geek co-workers.

She leaned against her desk, too pretty for her own good. "I read somewhere that men think about sex every six seconds."

"That's got to be an exaggeration. I've only thought about it twice today." He grinned at her. "After we did it."

She returned his smile, and he wished that he could trust her, that she wasn't Lady Savannah.

"So can you take time off for lunch?" he asked.

"It's a little early, but I suppose I could."

He motioned to her computer. "What were you working on?"

"I'm writing a manual for a system I designed."

"You don't look like a computer nerd."

She rolled her eyes. "That's such a cliché, Michael."

Oh, yeah? he thought. What about the Poindexter types he'd seen boxed up in their cubbyholes?

"There's a sandwich shop nearby. Is that okay with you?"

"Sure." She reached for her purse and slipped the strap over her shoulder. "I go there all the time."

Once they were outside, the sun glinted off Lea's hair. She'd styled it long and loose, but Michael hadn't given her much time to fuss with it this morning. His sexual appetite had gotten in the way.

They walked to the eatery and ordered chicken salad sandwiches and two tall plastic cups of lemonade. The young man working the counter gave Lea a special smile, and Michael felt a pang of possessiveness.

Not a good sign, he told himself.

They sat across from each other at a small white table. The sandwich shop offered a floor-to-ceiling view of Johnson Square, where financial advisers and bankers spent their workday.

Lea opened her potato chips and when she offered him one, feeding it to him, he started thinking about sex again, wondering if every six seconds wasn't too far off the mark.

The guy behind the counter looked disappointed, realizing, it seemed, that Lea and Michael were a couple, not co-workers.

Tough luck, Michael thought.

She sipped her lemonade and started in on her sandwich. He ate, too, considering she only had thirty minutes for lunch. He knew her daily schedule. He'd investigated every aspect of her professional life.

"This is good," she said. "I was hungrier than I thought."

"We missed breakfast."

"Yes, we did." She moistened her lips. "We were too busy to eat."

The every-six-seconds curse returned. "You're driving me crazy, Lea. Being with you is all I think about."

"Me, too."

Their gazes locked, and he knew he was in trouble. He'd never been this attracted to anyone before. Most of his relationships were over before they even started. Yet here he was, losing his common sense, getting sidetracked by a female who'd committed a psychological crime.

She smiled at him. "I'm glad you invited me to lunch. It was a nice surprise. Sort of romantic."

His heart clenched. He hadn't asked her to lunch to romance her. This was part of his job. "Actually, I was wondering if you'd like to help me with my case tonight." He paused, steeling the emotions she kept tying into knots. "There's no reason for us to wait until Saturday."

She broke eye contact. "Are you sure you need me to do this? I don't think I'm going to be much help."

"Sure you will," he said, hating this twisted game. "I already told you, I could really use a woman's perspective."

The beautiful, seductive woman who'd become his obsession, he thought. The lady leading him straight to hell.

# Six

Lea hadn't expected Michael to make their stalker investigation session so cozy. He'd placed a platter of fruit and cheese on the coffee table and encouraged her to have a glass of wine with him. So she sipped chardonnay and nibbled on apples and Brie, pretending she wasn't a nervous wreck.

"I guess I better start at the beginning." Michael plucked a grape and popped it into his mouth. "The first e-mail your father received was in February. It said, 'I've been watching you.' The second one that arrived said, 'You will suffer' and the third said, 'I'm still watching you.' All three were signed Lady Savannah."

When he searched her gaze, she forced herself to

remain calm, to keep her hands steady. "Did anything happen after that?"

Michael nodded. "In March, Lady Savannah sent him a virus that crashed his computer."

"How did you know it was from the same person? Was there a message attached?" she asked, hoping her questions sounded believable.

"Yes." He moved a little closer. They sat side by side on his sofa, the skylight above their heads reflecting a star-speckled evening. "The note said, 'Expect the unexpected. This isn't over.' That was her most cryptic message. Coupled with the virus, we knew she was serious." He paused. "What do you think 'This isn't over,' means, Lea?"

"I don't know." The wine hit her stomach like liquid fire. Could he tell she was lying? Was he assessing her body language? The way she shifted on the couch? "What do you think it means?"

"That she had something significant in store for Danforth, something that hasn't come to fruition yet."

She took another burning sip of the chardonnay. "Like what?"

"I haven't figured that out yet. But it's rather puzzling why so much time has passed without her contacting Danforth again." He ate another grape, contemplating the case. "It's got to be one of two things. She's waiting for the perfect opportunity to make her next move, or she changed her mind for some reason."

Yes, Lea thought. She changed her mind; she couldn't go through with it. "What do you know about Lady Savannah? What sort of details do you have?"

"I've worked out a profile on her." He reached for a file he'd left on the end table. "First of all, there are three types of stalkers. Low-threat, medium-threat and high-threat." He opened the folder and shuffled through the papers. "Lady Savannah is a medium-threat stalker. This type of stalker usually knows the principal, the person they're stalking."

"How well do they know them?"

"More often than not, the stalker has a disgruntled association with them, like an ex-lover, a former friend, an ex-business partner."

Or an abandoned child, she thought. A *my lai* who'd been left in Vietnam. "Are medium-threat stalkers dangerous?"

"They can be. The biggest danger is that they usually know a lot about the principal. They're not like a low-threat stalker who's just trying to get close to the principal, hoping to attract his attention, like an adoring fan. Medium-threat stalkers have a stronger agenda and are more suspect in their motives."

Guilty, Lea took a deep breath. She'd threatened her father to get back at him, to make him pay for her pain. "What about high-threat stalkers?"

"They're severely dangerous, but Lady Savannah doesn't fit that profile. High-threat stalkers are delusional, men and women living in a fantasy world. They usually have a history of mental illness and are obsessed with the principal. They don't have any regard for the law, and they don't care about the consequences."

"But Lady Savannah does?"

"Yes." He tasted the Brie. "She was cautious in her approach. I think she lives and works in the mainstream world and doesn't want her life ruined by a police inquiry or a restraining order. She cares if she gets caught."

"Are the police involved in this investigation?" she asked, her heart pounding against her breast.

"Damn straight they are. Danforth is running for state senator. He isn't leaving anything to chance, which is why he brought me in on the stalking case."

Lea fell silent, wondering what Michael would say if she told him the truth, if she admitted why she'd sent the virus and what "This isn't over" meant. Would he forgive her? Or would he look upon her with disdain?

Anxious, she glanced up to find him watching her. "Do the police have a description of Lady Savannah? Has anyone seen her?"

"Yes." He broke eye contact and paged through the file again. "Her e-mail messages were traced to public computers. First a local library, then two different copy centers and finally an Internet café, where the virus was sent."

"And the employees at these places remember her?"

"The manager at the Internet café does." He handed Lea a sketch of Lady Savannah. "It's a crude likeness, but it's all we have."

She studied the drawing, grateful it didn't resemble her. "Mid- to late-twenties, with auburn hair and tinted glasses."

"Exactly. But I've come to the conclusion that

her hair was a wig, and that the glasses played a bigger part in her disguise than the police realized."

Lea wasn't about to ask him to expound on why Lady Savannah needed to mask her eyes.

"I think her height was altered, too," he went on to say. "That she was wearing platform shoes, but the hem of her pants was too long for the manager to notice. He said she was tall and slim, like a model, but I don't think that's correct."

"You think she's short and plump?"

He raised his eyebrows at that. "I think the shoes gave her the illusion of being model-like. She's obviously lean enough to be considered slim and the extra height made her look even thinner."

Lea recalled the manager at the Internet café, recalling the way he'd checked her out. "Do you think he likes tall, thin girls? Do you think that's why he remembers her?"

"Yes, that's exactly what I think. He gave us a better description of her body than her face."

"So she could be anyone? Anyone who's had an association with my father?"

"Anyone with cause to threaten him," Michael corrected.

"Yes, of course." She returned the sketch, wanting him to bury it in the file, to hide it from view.

But he didn't. He kept the drawing in his hand. "I think she's computer savvy. That she wrote the virus herself."

"If she's so computer savvy, why did she use public computers?"

"Because she wanted the e-mails to get traced.

And she wanted to be seen. She was trying to create a false description of Lady Savannah."

Her palms began to sweat. "Maybe you're wrong, Michael. Maybe she really is a tall, slim redhead."

He shook his head. "It was just a clever disguise."

Maybe so, Lea thought. But Lady Savannah was a coward, unable to admit the truth, to let her lover turn her over to the police.

"I've investigated every angle of this case," he said. "In the beginning, I even suspected John Van Gelder, your father's opponent. I thought maybe Van Gelder hired the stalker as a ruse to scare Danforth into withdrawing from the race." He glanced at the sketch. "But this isn't about dirty politics."

She didn't respond. Because, like Michael, she knew John Van Gelder didn't have anything to do with her father's stalker. Lea Nguyen was Lady Savannah.

John Van Gelder gazed out the window, peering at the moonlit walkway and grassy perimeter of the yard. The boxy little house belonged to Hayden Murphy, a member of his advisory team.

Hayden was a kid, as far as John was concerned. Twenty-three, the same age as John's daughter.

Releasing an exhausted sigh, he turned away from the window and found Hayden watching him. The kid was on a low rung on the political ladder, but he wasn't as opinionated as the seasoned members of the team. He did as he was told.

"You look troubled," Hayden said.

"Gee, I wonder why."

"I'm digging as deep as I can, sir."

"Well, dig deeper. Find some dirt on Danforth." John intended to win the senatorial race, even if it meant slinging a crap-load of mud. "Find something to tarnish that Honest Abe image of his. Something tabloid-worthy."

"I will. I promise I will."

John squinted at Hayden. With his blond hair and fraternity-boy features, he looked more like a university student than an adviser, reminding John that his daughter had completed her European college studies this year.

John was a widower, and Selene was his only child. Would he be so damn driven to win this race if he'd had a son?

Not a son like Hayden, he thought. So far, the ambitious young yes-man hadn't uncovered one shred of scandalous information. John really needed something to discredit his opponent. He'd spent most of his life believing that he was the second choice to Abraham Danforth and he wasn't about to come in second this time.

Frustrated, he turned his attention back to Hayden. "Maybe you're not ready for a job of this caliber."

The younger man squared his shoulders. "That isn't true. I'll get what you're looking for."

"You better," John threatened. "Because if you don't, I'll find someone who will."

Lea cleared the half-eaten fruit and cheese platter and Michael gathered the empty wine glasses. They went into the kitchen together, but their conversation was stilted, the Lady Savannah session leaving them tense.

He set their glasses in the sink, and she studied apple slices that had already begun to brown. The grapes were salvageable, but that was the least of Michael's concerns. Lea certainly seemed preoccupied with the task, making more of her kitchen duty than necessary.

"Don't worry about that," he said.

She looked up. "I don't believe in wasting food."

Because she knew what it was like to go hungry, he thought. "Fine. Whatever. Save it all if you want to." He'd been hoping for a confession from her, yet here she was, fussing over their wilted snack, giving a few measly apple slices her undivided attention.

He glanced at the clock, noting it was bedtime. "You seem uptight."

She bagged the fruit, her movements a bit too jittery. "It's been a long day. Maybe I just need to relax." She opened the fridge and ducked her head. "Maybe I just need you to hold me."

To alleviate her guilt? he wondered. Or to work up the courage to tell him the truth? "You should move into my room."

"Are you sure?" She closed the fridge and turned to face him, her eyes full of hope. "If you'd rather keep your privacy."

"It doesn't make sense for us to have separate rooms." And being affectionate with her would help his cause, wouldn't it? "We're already involved."

She gave him a shaky smile. "Yes, we are."

He helped her transfer her clothes into his closet,

and he realized this was the first time he'd come close to having a live-in lover. Two weeks wasn't much, but considering the circumstances, it felt like a monumental commitment.

Side by side, they got ready for bed, brushing their teeth and changing into sleeping attire. He chose a pair of drawstring shorts, and she put on a virginal-looking nightgown.

They climbed into bed, and he turned out the light. The room wasn't overly dark. A low-hung moon cast a romantic glow over the sheets.

Lea moved closer, and he slipped his arms around her. She rested her head on his shoulder, her hair tickling his chin.

"Thank you, Michael."

"For what?"

"For holding me."

"Sure." He told himself he didn't have a choice. Being near her was his only option. She sighed, and he knew she wasn't going to confess her sin, at least not tonight.

"Tell me about being Seminole," she said. "You haven't taught me about your heritage yet."

He considered what to say. He wanted to tell her something pretty, something that made the pain from his childhood more bearable. "According to Seminole legend, the Creator, the grandfather of all things, created the Earth and everything on it. He made sure that certain animals and plants possessed healing powers. But he chose Panther to walk the Earth first."

"Really? Why?"

"Panther was his favorite. He said Panther was majestic and beautiful, with patience and strength."

Michael paused, his memories drifting back to his youth. "My mother told me about that because we're from the Panther clan."

Lea seemed intrigued. "I always thought of panthers as fierce."

"My mom was fierce when she got angry at my father." He sighed. "Infidelity isn't common among the Seminole. She never even considered that her husband would cheat on her."

She adjusted the sheet draped around their hips. "I feel sad for her."

He shrugged, even though his emotions had turned tight. "It's over. She's gone now."

"But she's still part of who you are, Michael."

That much he couldn't deny. He was his mother's son, but he hadn't been able to save her, to shake his two-timing father from her blood.

When he fell silent, Lea snuggled closer to him. "Did your mother ever cook Seminole meals for you?"

"Sometimes she made pumpkin soup. It was my favorite."

She snuggled closer. "Do you think you could duplicate the recipe? Maybe teach me how to make it?"

Could he? He used to sit at the kitchen table and watch while it was being prepared. "I can try. From what I recall, my mother used to add extra nutmeg and sugar to it."

She smiled. "No wonder it was your favorite."

He linked his fingers through hers and brought their joined hands to his lips, brushing her knuckles with a soft kiss. "I do have a bit of a sweet tooth."

She shifted in his arms, and when she put her head against his chest, he knew she was listening to the rhythm of his heart. Like rain falling on a metal roof, he thought. "I've never been to the reservation where my mom grew up. That's crazy, isn't it? I've never seen my mother's homeland."

"Then you should go there someday."

"I should. But my mom had a falling out with her family. It would probably be awkward." He glanced up at the ceiling and saw shadows above his head. "The Seminole are a matriarchal society, but my father didn't respect that."

"Yet your mother married him."

"I think she wanted him because he was forbidden to her. Her parents didn't want their daughter to make eye contact with Stan Whittaker, let alone marry him."

"Stan? That was his name?"

He nodded. "My mom's name was Peggy Ann Tiger."

"Is Tiger a common family name?"

"You mean among my mother's people? It seems to be."

"In Vietnam, her name would be Tiger Ann Peggy," Lea said. "A family name comes first, then a middle name, then the first. But that doesn't mean you refer to someone by his or her last name. You use their given name."

He pondered their conversation for a moment. "Do given names have special meaning?"

"Most do. Lan means orchid. Sometimes I buy orchids at the flower shop to remember my mother."

"Do you have a picture of her?" he asked.

"Just one. Taken with my father. Nearly everything in her village was destroyed, but she found that picture among the rubble." Lea's voice turned sad. "It was all she had left."

He stroked the length of her hair, comforting her, comforting himself. "I have a few pictures of my parents. But I don't know why I saved the ones of my dad."

"For the same reason I saved the photo my father is in. You knew it would've mattered to your mother."

He wanted to point out that Abraham Danforth was a better man than Stan Whittaker, but he doubted Lea would agree. She'd threatened her father, something Michael would have never done.

Then again, maybe he...

He what? Should have stalked his old man? Made the bastard fear for his life? He blew out a rough breath, knowing his mind was taking him down a dangerous path, trying to find ways to condone Lea's crime.

"Are you all right?" She reached up to skim his cheek, and suddenly the room turned dark, moonlight fading from the bed.

Emotional déjà vu, he thought, as his heart thundered in his chest. "I'm fine," he managed. "Just fine," he added, as she rolled over to kiss him, making everything but the sweet, warm taste of her disappear.

# Seven

**W**hittaker and Associates was encased in a single-level, freestanding structure, with parking lot access and double-glass doors.

Lea told herself to relax, but her guilt kept getting in the way. She should be arriving at Michael's office to turn herself in instead of bringing him a sugary snack.

She let out the breath she was holding and entered the building. The lobby was vast, with a black-and-white tiled floor and a marble reception desk. Leather couches and brass accent tables offered a modern seating arrangement, and original works of art added splashes of bold, bright color.

Anxious, Lea approached the reception desk, but

the middle-aged woman manning the attractive workstation was already aware of her.

"Good afternoon." The woman gave her a pleasant smile. She wore wire-rimmed glasses and her ash-brown hair was cut in a sleek, professional style. "May I help you?"

"I'm looking for Michael Whittaker."

"Mr. Whittaker isn't in. Would you like to schedule an appointment to see him for another time?"

Lea hadn't considered the possibly that Michael wouldn't be in his office at this hour. "No, thank you."

Just then, the door beside the reception desk opened and Cindy emerged, wearing a stunning black suit, her golden-blond hair coiled into a soft chignon. Her skirt rode above her knees, showcasing long, shapely legs. When she moved forward, her shoes hit the floor like a round of well-aimed bullets, ringing in Lea's ears.

Cindy answered that ring with a wide-eyed expression. "Well, hello, Lea. How nice to see you."

"It's nice to see you, too." She noticed the receptionist had gone back to work, giving them the illusion of a private conversation. "I stopped by to visit Michael, but he isn't in." She shifted the pastry box in her hand. "I'll catch him later."

"No, no. Don't rush off. He should be back shortly." Cindy gestured to the door from which she'd emerged. "Have some coffee with me. I'm due for a break."

Lea thought it would be rude to refuse, so she followed the blonde to her office, which was just as chic as the lobby, with the same leather-and-chrome decor.

"How about decaffeinated cappuccino?" Cindy asked, without bothering to wait for an answer. She went about making the gourmet brew, filling the room with the hiss of frothing milk.

Lea took a chair, unable to admit that she rarely drank coffee.

"There. Now isn't this divine?" Cindy placed an oversize mug in front of her. "Don't you just love cappuccino? It's too late in the day for caffeine, though. Don't you agree?"

"Yes, I suppose it is." She lifted the pastry box from her lap. "I brought a snack for Michael, but there's plenty if you'd like one."

"Oh, let's see." The blonde peered inside. "That's quite a selection."

"Michael told me he had a sweet tooth."

Cindy looked up with a slow, Southern smile. "I'll just bet he does." She declined a pastry and drank her coffee instead.

Lea wasn't sure what to make of the sexual innuendo. She was still getting accustomed to women like Cindy. There weren't any brazen blondes in Vietnam, at least not within the sphere of her *my lai* existence.

"I know who you are," Cindy said.

"Excuse me?"

"I know you're Abraham Danforth's daughter. But I'm the only person at Whittaker and Associates who knows. Besides Michael, of course."

"He must trust you."

"I'm in charge of making sure your story doesn't hit the tabloids." Cindy sat back in her chair. "What puzzles me is why you won't allow Mr. Danforth to call a press conference. If it's handled correctly, it won't end up on the front page of some tacky gossip rag."

"I'm not ready to face the media. And I'm not sure I ever will be."

"Your father is a fascinating man. Wildly handsome, too. I can't imagine turning away from him. I think you're a fortunate young woman."

Lea didn't know what to say, so she drank her cappuccino and kept quiet.

"Have you ever seen Crofthaven?" the blonde asked. "Who wouldn't want to be associated with a seaside mansion like that? I simply love old money." She laughed a little. "I love new money, too."

"That doesn't matter to me." Lea supposed she couldn't fault Cindy for being honest, but she still wasn't comfortable around Michael's gorgeous assistant.

"Are you familiar with The Landings?" the other woman asked.

"The gated community on Skidaway Island?"

"Exactly. Golf courses, tennis courts, a fitness club. I used to live there with my boyfriend until he kicked me out." Cindy tossed her head and sent the diamond-studded hoops in her ears dancing. "But it doesn't matter because I'm interested in someone else now."

Who? Lea wondered. Abraham Danforth? Was it possible that Cindy had set her sights on Lea's father?

"Speaking of someone else..." The blonde released a sensual sigh. "That boss of mine is certainly a working girl's dream." She leaned in close. "How lucky are you?"

The coffee burned Lea's stomach like acid. "Michael told you about us?"

"That you're sharing his bed?" The earrings spun again. "He didn't have to. I saw you two at the gallery, remember? And I've been around him long enough to sense these things."

Lea fought the urge to frown, to make her displeasure known. Why should Cindy care whom her boss was sleeping with? And why did she feel compelled to mention it?

"My, my." The other woman glanced at the door and smiled. "Speak of the devil. Look who just popped his head in."

Lea spun around to see Michael. He met her gaze, and her coffee-riddled stomach unleashed a horde of decaffeinated butterflies.

"Speak of the devil," he mimicked. "Were you ladies talking about me?"

Cindy rose from her chair and made an elegant sweep across the room. "You mean you didn't hear us?"

"No, I can't say that I did."

"Well, then, we're not going to tell you what we said. Are we, Lea?"

Instead of indulging Cindy's game, Lea walked toward Michael, offering him a lover's smile. "I got off work early, so I stopped by to see you. To bring you some pastries."

He smiled at her. "That sounds good. I'm about ready to call it a day."

Lea turned to Cindy. "Thank you for the cappuccino."

"Don't mention it." The blonde watched them depart without another word.

Lea and Michael left in separate cars and by the time they arrived at his house, he was just curious enough to question her. But she expected as much.

"So what were you and Cindy talking about?"

"This and that." She went into the kitchen and removed two dessert plates from the cupboard. "Which one would you like?" She opened the pastry box and extended it to him.

He chose a chocolate éclair. "Come on. What'd you talk about?"

She handed him a fork. "Cindy told me that she knew I was Abraham's daughter. But I guess you had to tell her."

"That's right, I did. Cindy always handles media control."

Lea reached for an apple fritter, wishing she trusted Michael's administrative assistant as much as he did. "Is she working on the stalking investigation, too?"

"No." A frown furrowed his brow. "That's my area of expertise."

"So you haven't discussed Lady Savannah with her?"

"No," he said again. "I haven't."

Silence stretched between them, a reminder that their relationship was based on a lie. But even so, Lea knew Michael didn't have any evidence on her. If he did, he would have confronted her by now.

She glanced at her plate, knowing she owed him the truth. But in this case, the truth wouldn't set her free. She would lose the man she loved.

"What are you thinking about?" he asked.

You, she wanted to say. And how sorry she was to keep deceiving him. But how could she look him in the eye and admit that she was a stalker? Just the term alone shamed her.

"Lea?" he pressed.

"I'm not thinking about anything."

"Then tell me what else you and Cindy discussed."

She wasn't about to repeat the blonde's flattering remarks about him. The other woman's flamboyant manner was already rubbing her the wrong way. "I think Cindy's interested in my father."

He started. "You mean romantically?"

"It fits, doesn't it? He's rich and powerful and handsome. And you said you thought her mystery man might be one of your colleagues. So why not a client?"

"I suppose it's possible." He finally cut into the éclair. "But I doubt it will do her any good. I think Danforth has feelings for his campaign manager."

This time Lea started. She hadn't expected her father to have a woman in his life. "What's her name?"

"Nicola Granville. But I'm not positive about this. I just get a vibe whenever I see them together." He stopped eating to look at her. "But some people have that tangible kind of chemistry."

"Almost as if you can touch it?"

He moved closer. "Yes."

"Like us?"

"Yes," he said again, leaning in to kiss her, to slide his hands through her hair.

She melted against him, and he unbuttoned the

front of her blouse. His hands were warm and strong and possessive. When he unzipped her skirt, she wondered if he could sense that she loved him, if he had any idea that he'd captured her soul.

He ended the kiss, and they stared at each other. She was partially undressed, and his breathing was hard and labored.

"You taste like chocolate," she said.

"And you taste like everything I shouldn't have." He pushed her skirt down. "Everything I want." He snapped the elastic on her panty hose. "Take those damn things off."

She leveled her gaze. "You're demanding."

"And you're messing with my brain." He pinned her against the counter. "Just take them off."

"Why should I?" she challenged, even though her knees had gone as weak as her heart.

"Because it's what I want."

She tilted her chin. "Then do it yourself."

That was all it took. He grabbed her nylons and literally tore them from her body, but Lea didn't care. She needed to feel his passion, the desperation that drew him to her.

Struggling for balance, she closed her eyes, and he dropped to the floor, kneeling in front of her. When he yanked her panties down, her pulse pounded like a rawhide drum.

"Do you know where it is, Lea?"

She opened her eyes. "What?"

"The hidden camera."

Properly stunned, she froze. "Michael—"

He seized her hips and pulled her against his mouth.

Heat slammed through her system and she pitched forward, gasping for her next breath. Was the camera running? Was he filming her surrender? The idea shocked her. But it aroused her, too.

He tasted her, deep and slow, and she couldn't stop the pleasure—the forbidden wetness, the sweet, spiraling sensation.

Lea moved against his mouth, wanting to remember this feeling forever. She'd never imagined that being in love could be so erotic. He did wicked things to her, and she traced his features, memorizing him in her mind, using the tips of her fingers.

"Do you want more?" he asked.

"Yes." So much more. Need rushed through her veins, spilling like a luminous fountain. Colors blurred, then separated, streaking across her heart.

Giving her what she wanted, he heightened each kiss. She lost the battle and shuddered against him, yielding to her emotions, to an orgasm as slick and moist as the pressure between her legs.

He came to his feet and she fell into his arms, her body still quaking, colors still spinning.

"Lea?"

"Hmm?"

"The camera isn't on."

She blinked through the kaleidoscope behind her eyes. "I wouldn't have cared if it was."

He gave her a masculine smile. "I know."

She held on to his shoulders, regaining her senses. "You're cocky, Michael."

"Am I?" He took her hand and rubbed it against his fly.

"Yes, you most certainly are." She unzipped his

trousers and suddenly their flirtation turned to frustration, to something neither of them could deny.

He was angry at himself for needing her so badly, she thought, as he pushed his tongue into her mouth, devouring her in one fell swoop, making her head spin.

He removed a condom from his wallet and fought to open the package, anxious to thrust into her, to take what he wished he didn't want. Lea had no intention of stopping him. She let him curse in her ear, knowing it wouldn't change the passion that was about to erupt.

He bit the side of her neck, becoming her vampire once again. She yanked off his clothes, and they made love like maniacal bloodsuckers, until they ended up on the kitchen floor, nearly bruising each other's skin.

She wrapped her legs and around him and he braced his arms above her, kissing her hard and fast. She could taste herself on his lips, a flavor that only added to the frenzy.

Their worlds were colliding, crashing like shattered glass. But that didn't seem to matter. Not now, not while they were naked, not while he was moving inside her.

"This is going to happen fast," he said.

"I don't care." She scraped her nails down his back and felt his spine shiver.

"Neither do I." He pumped even harder, filling her as deeply and desperately as he could.

They climaxed at the same time, at the very same instant, gasping into each other mouths, their hearts beating wildly.

When it was over, when Lea could see through the blinding haze, she knew their words were a lie. They both cared, far too much.

On Saturday morning, Michael paced Clay's office. The other man sat on the edge of his desk in a T-shirt, frayed jeans and sleep-tousled hair. Michael had awakened him with a cell phone call, and the club owner was still feeling the effects of his late-night work hours.

"I'm sorry," Michael said. "I shouldn't have bothered you."

"What are friends for?" Clay scrubbed his hand across his jaw. "Besides, it's no big deal for me to meet you here."

"No, I suppose not." Michael stopped pacing to face his friend. Clay had a loft-style apartment above the club. He lived and worked at Steam. "Is your fiancée still asleep?"

"No. The phone woke her up, too."

"She must think I'm a pain in the ass. Calling you at this hour."

"Naw. She just thinks you're in love."

Michael scowled. "I suppose that's what you think, too?"

The other man walked over to a wet bar and removed a carton of orange juice, pouring two glasses. He spiked Michael's with vodka and handed it to him. "You know damn well I do."

"Well, you're wrong." He accepted the screwdriver and took a long, hard swallow, knowing he needed it.

"If you say so." Clay settled in with his orange juice, resuming a spot on his mahogany desk.

Michael refused to entertain thoughts of love, to let his mind take him in that direction. Yet he couldn't keep going on the way he was, holding Lea each night, wanting her, waiting for his heart to explode. "I came up with a plan to trap her."

"Is that what brought you here at this ungodly hour?"

"Yes, but I feel like I'm betraying her."

"Makes a person wonder why."

"Knock off the love crap. I'm guilty because I'm sleeping with her." And cuddling with her, he thought. And having sex on the kitchen floor.

Clay shook his head. "I wish you hadn't gotten involved with her."

Beyond frustrated, Michael poured himself another drink, adding an extra shot of vodka, not giving a damn that he was having alcohol for breakfast. "What if my plan to trap her only makes things worse?"

"How much worse can it be? You're already an emotional mess. She's already getting to you."

"I'm going to lose her. Once I turn her in, it's going to be over." Michael blew out a ragged breath, squinting in the dim light. The blinds on the windows were drawn, shutting out the sun, matching his mood. "There's a part of me that wishes I could forget about what she did. Pretend it never happened. Tell Danforth the case is getting cold and probably won't be solved."

"I'm not going to comment on that. Whatever you decide is up to you."

"I'm going through with my plan." Because he needed to hear Lea's confession. He needed her to take responsibility for her actions. "I can't obstruct justice."

"When is this going to happen, Mike?"

His chest turned tight. "Today. This afternoon. I've already got everything ready to go."

"Then I'm not going to ask you what the plan is."

"No, there's no point. I didn't come here to discuss the specifics. I just needed to get it off my chest. To say it out loud." To convince himself to go through with it, he thought. To trap Lea into telling him the truth.

# Eight

"**W**hy won't you tell me where we're going?" Lea asked.

Michael checked his rearview mirror. He wasn't sure if he was being a conscientious driver or avoiding his lover's gaze. "You'll see when we get there."

"You're being so secretive, Michael."

He merely nodded. Giving her information ahead of time wouldn't work in his favor.

Silent, he continued driving. Their final destination was located in the vicinity of Savannah State University, and he knew Lea would recognize the side streets once they got closer. But would she say anything? Or would she pretend the area was unfamiliar?

They stopped at a red light and he could feel her

watching him. Wondering, he assumed, what the hell he was up to. He turned toward her and, for a moment, they simply stared at each other. He wanted to reach out, to skim her cheek, but touching her would only make him ache.

"The light's green."

"What?"

"The light."

"Oh, of course." He engaged the gas pedal and sped across the intersection. He was still a bit hungover from earlier, from drinking screwdrivers at seven in the morning.

"I wish you'd tell me where we're going," she said.

"You'll find out soon enough." He'd never expected a woman to affect him so badly, to make such a mess out of his neat and orderly life.

By the time they arrived at the Internet café, tension brimmed like steam in a pressure cooker. He suspected Lea had begun to sweat.

"What are we doing here?" she asked.

He parked the car. "I'm going to interview the manager about Lady Savannah."

She gazed out the windshield, refusing to look at him, refusing to unbuckle her seat belt. "But you've already done that. He already gave you a description of her."

"I want to talk to him again."

She remained motionless. "Then I'll wait here."

Michael prepared to exit the vehicle, knowing he was doing the right thing and hating himself for it. "You can't. I need your help."

"That doesn't make sense."

"Sure it does." He flipped the automatic lock on the trunk and got out of the car. "Come on. I'll show you what I mean."

Lea finally budged and followed him to the back of the Mercedes. He removed a handled shopping bag and presented it to her.

She peered inside and saw the auburn-colored wig. Instantly, her skin paled.

"It's almost identical to the one Lady Savannah wore," he said. "There's a pair of platform shoes in there, too. Oh, and tinted glasses." He reached into the bag and removed the plastic-rimmed specs. "I bought these at an optometrist downtown. They're the same shape as the glasses she had on."

"You're going to show all of this to the manager?" she asked, her voice barely audible.

"No." He kept his gaze locked onto hers, pinning her in place. "You're going to dress up as Lady Savannah for me."

She didn't respond; she didn't utter one quavering word. Silence stretched between them, like a motionless gap in time. When she attempted to return the bag to him, he refused take it. Instead he waited for her to speak, the midafternoon sun beating brutally on his back. But Lea fared much worse. She looked as though she were wilting, fading right before his eyes.

"I can't do this, Michael."

He blinked, losing sight of her for a second, wishing he didn't feel like a ruthless bastard, wishing she hadn't put him in this position. "Why not?"

"I just can't."

"Why not?" he asked again, his tone harsher this time.

Her body swayed. "You know why."

"Do I?"

"Yes." She dropped the bag and it hit the ground with a clunk, landing on its side, spilling the lid to the shoebox. The wig fell out, too. For an instant, it looked like dried blood on the pavement. "I'm her, Michael. I'm Lady Savannah."

His heart picked up speed. He'd been waiting to hear her say those words out loud, waiting for the truth. "You sent the virus?" He gestured to the Internet café. "It was you the manager saw that day?"

"Yes." She glanced at the fallen articles. "I wore a wig like that. And platform shoes and glasses. But I bought everything in California. Before I came to Savannah."

She teetered on her feet, the way she'd done on the night of the fund-raiser. Michael feared she might faint. The weather was unbearably hot, the air much too sticky.

"Get back in the car," he told her.

She didn't argue, but he shadowed her just the same, preparing to catch her if she passed out. When she was secure in her seat, he picked up the fallen bag and climbed behind the wheel. She glanced over at him, and he started the engine, running the air conditioner to cool her off.

Her hair blew gently around her face, making her look soft and vulnerable. Michael cursed his attraction to her.

"You're not going to make me go into the café?" she asked.

He shook his head.

She blew out a shaky breath. "You don't need the manager to identify me?"

He let the car idle, choosing to remain where they were. He wasn't ready to pull into traffic yet. "You already confessed."

"Will you take me home?" She leaned her head against the seat rest. Her skin was still pale and her hair still fluttered around her face. Even her blouse gave her a lost quality. It was made of crinkled cotton, sheer enough to expose the outline of her bra.

"I'll take you to my house." He put the car into gear. "You have a lot of explaining to do, Lea."

"Are you going to turn me in?"

Michael exited the parking lot. He didn't want to discuss his actions with her. Hell, he didn't even want to look at her. He didn't want to see the fear in her eyes.

Those beautiful Amerasian eyes, he thought.

He couldn't allow himself to think of her as a wounded mixed blood. A half-breed. *Con lai.* He had to think of her as Lady Savannah, the woman who'd threatened Abraham Danforth, the stalker Michael had been tracking.

Michael drove Lea to his house, and she went straight to the refrigerator and poured a glass of orange juice, hoping to stabilize her blood sugar. She hadn't expected him to trap her into a confession, to leave her weak-limbed and shaky.

"You okay?" he asked.

She sipped the juice and nodded. He was being attentive, but not in a warm, caring way. The man watching her was cool and cautious. But she could hardly blame him. Why should he trust her?

"Can we go to the game room?" she asked.

He raised his eyebrows. "Why? Do you want to challenge me to a game of pool? Wager on whether or not I'll turn you in?"

Her chest constricted. "No. I want to play some music on the jukebox." Something to calm her nerves, something soft and familiar.

"Be my guest." He gestured, indicating for her to lead the way.

Once they were in the game room, she scanned the jukebox, making her selections, choosing classic love songs.

Michael didn't comment. He got himself a bottled soda and settled onto a bar stool. He looked tired, she thought. Hard-edged and exhausted.

"I never meant to hurt you," she said. To drag him into her sordid existence.

"But you meant to hurt your dad." He removed the cap on his cola and tossed it into a trash can beside the bar. "You meant to threaten him."

"Yes, but it took years for my hatred to build, years of hoping and praying that he would return to Vietnam someday, that he hadn't forgotten about my mother." She sat on a futon couch near the window. The room was decorated with casual furnishings, offering seating arrangements around the pool table and air hockey game table. "When I was in the refugee camp in the Philippines, I struggled with my hatred. The camp was filled with other Amerasians and most of them still had hope of finding their fathers and being accepted into their lives. And deep down, I wanted to feel that way, too."

"So when did you start hating Danforth enough to threaten him?"

"After I came to America and discovered that he'd been married when he slept with my mother, that he had other children." She sipped her juice, combating the dryness in her mouth. "My mother told me that he was injured when they'd met, that he was struggling with his memory. But she never entertained the possibility that he could have been married."

Michael leaned forward. "Why not?"

"Because she said he wasn't the kind of man who would forget that he had a wife. No matter how injured he was."

"Amnesia doesn't work that way."

"It can. Some people have selective amnesia. Besides, he told my mother his first name." She glanced out the window, tears fogging her eyes. "That much Abraham knew about himself."

"Maybe so, but he didn't remember that he was married. It wasn't his fault."

"It felt like his fault to me. He seemed like a liar and a cheat."

Michael turned quiet, and Lea took a ragged breath. When another song began to play, the lyrics drifted like childhood ghosts, floating between them, making her eyes water even more. But even so, she knew there was nothing left to say in her defense. Threatening her father was wrong.

"What did the note with the virus mean?" Michael asked.

Shame coiled around her heart. "Expect the unexpected? This isn't over?"

"Exactly. Explain that to me."

"It meant what you assumed it did. That Lady Savannah had something specific in mind for Abraham Danforth."

"Which was?"

"Destroying his political career at a public event, announcing to the world that Honest Abe had cheated on his wife, that he'd abandoned a child in Vietnam."

Michael frowned. "And that public event turned out to be the July Fourth fund-raiser?"

"Yes. I attended the fund-raiser with a synchronized plan. First, I would confront Abraham and tell him who I was. Then, while his head was still reeling from the news, I would make the same announcement at the podium, letting everyone know that he was a liar and a cheat."

"But you never approached the podium." He glanced up and snared her gaze. "You started shaking instead."

"Because Abraham didn't react the way I'd expected. He didn't deny that I could be his daughter. He didn't even try to defend himself. And I could tell he wasn't lying when he said that he thought my mother had died when her village was destroyed." Lea held Michael's gaze, even though it was difficult to look at him, to know he was judging her. "At that point, it was all I could do to remain standing, to stop myself from falling apart."

He closed his eyes, and she sensed he was thinking about the way she'd cried in his arms that night, the way they'd touched and kissed and made sweet, desperate love.

"Are you sorry for what you did?" he asked.

"For threatening my father?" She crossed her arms, hugging herself, wishing Michael would hold her instead. "I'm extremely sorry. If I could take it back, I would."

He shifted in his seat. "Did you honestly think that you'd get away with it? That someone wouldn't connect Lady Savannah to you?"

"I didn't leave any evidence, so what proof would there be? I thought I was safe."

"And you were." He paused to finish his drink, to push away the bottle, to leave streaks across the lacquered bar top. "Until you started sleeping with me."

Yes, she thought. She'd gotten too close to her father's bodyguard, too close to the man investigating the case. "I don't regret being with you."

"Even now? After I trapped you?"

"That doesn't change how I feel." She couldn't make herself stop loving him. She couldn't turn off her emotions. "This is part of your job."

"And now here we are. The stalker and the detective." When the music stopped, he glanced at the jukebox. "We never really got the chance to enjoy each other's company. Not the way a regular couple would."

She understood what he meant, but they couldn't change the nature of their relationship, not after what she'd done. "Are you going to turn me in?"

"Yes," he responded. "But not to the police. I've decided to leave that up to your father."

She reached for a decorative pillow and held it against her heart, against the thundering beats. "Do you think he'll press charges?"

"I have no idea."

"What are you going to say to him?"

"I'm going to tell him the truth."

"When?" she asked, her heart still pounding.

"Today. Right now." Michael rose from his chair. "And you're coming with me."

Lea changed her clothes four times, which made no sense. It was too late to make an impression on her father, yet she was determined to look nice.

Michael probably thought she was crazy.

And what would Abraham Danforth think? she wondered. What would he think once he learned the truth? That Lea Nguyen was Lady Savannah?

"I don't want to do this," she said, wishing she could bolt, but knowing there was nowhere to run, nowhere to hide. "I don't want to face him."

"You don't have a choice." Michael steered the car toward Crofthaven, a magnificent Georgian-style mansion just outside Savannah. Along the way, oaks festooned with Spanish moss made a glorious presentation.

When the white-columned house came into view, Lea's anxiety worsened. She didn't want to feel like a frightened little girl with rock welts on her body, but how could she feel strong and secure? Worthy of being Abraham Danforth's daughter after what she'd done?

*"Bui doi,"* she said.

Michael turned to look at her. "What?"

*"Bui doi.* It means dust of life. The poorest of the poor."

His expression softened. "Is that what you were in Vietnam?"

"No. But many *my lai* children were. They lived on the streets. They committed crimes. They took drugs. They became prostitutes. They were the underbelly of society." She smoothed her skirt, fidgeting with the carefully ironed fabric. "My mother did everything she could to stop that from happening to me."

"Lan must have been an exceptional woman."

"Yes. But now I've shamed her. I've dishonored her memory."

He parked in an exquisite driveway. "Because you committed a crime?"

Lea nodded. "Against my father, no less."

He frowned at her. "That doesn't make you the dust of life."

."Then what does it make me?" she asked, gazing into his eyes and watching the afternoon light shift in their depths.

When he didn't respond, her heart turned sad. She wasn't the poorest of the poor, living in the bowels of society, yet she'd behaved as though she were.

"Let's go," he said. "I called ahead. Danforth is expecting us."

She stood on the massive porch with Michael, the mansion looming over her. "Did you warn him what this meeting was about?"

"No. I just said it was important."

She took a deep breath. Flowers bloomed, scenting the air with sweet, sunlit fragrances.

A housekeeper opened the front door and a few minutes later, Lea and Michael waited in a sitting room rife with antiques, two glasses of freshly squeezed lemonade at their disposal.

To Lea, Abraham's home was a Southern castle, with crystal and china and a collection of what she assumed were real Fabergé eggs displayed on a glass shelf.

As a child, she'd assumed all Americans were rich, but her young *my lai* view of rich couldn't compare to the trappings of a place like Crofthaven.

"How are you holding up?" Michael asked.

"Fine," she lied. She'd never been this nervous before, not even on the day she'd arrived in the States.

When Abraham Danforth entered the room, Michael stepped forward to greet him. The men shook hands, and Lea noticed that Michael, at six-two, stood several inches taller than her father, but Abraham's wide shoulders made him seem equally strong.

He turned to look at her, and her heart crawled straight to her throat, nearly blocking her windpipe. Abraham was a charismatic man, with dark brown hair and stunning blue eyes.

"Lea." He said her name and smiled. "I'm pleased to see you."

"You won't be," she managed, as she came to her feet. "Not after Michael tells you why we're here."

The politician made a perplexed face and addressed his bodyguard. "What's going on?"

"Your daughter is Lady Savannah," Michael said.

The air in Abraham's lungs whooshed out, and Lea flinched, wishing she could die a thousand sword-tipped deaths. Abraham's capable shoulders turned rigid and anger blazed in his eyes. He spun around to stare at her and she felt horribly sick inside.

"You sent those notes? That virus?"

"Yes."

"Why? Why would you do that me? To my family?"

"I wanted to hurt you. To destroy your political career."

"I never suspected you." He shook his head. "I never even considered the possibility. Do you hate me that much, Lea?"

"I did. But I don't anymore." Because she was afraid her legs wouldn't hold her, she sat on an ornate settee and looked up at him. "I thought you used my mother."

He didn't move. He simply stood before her, the light from several windows bathing him in a soft, summer glow. But even so, he remained big and powerful. "Is that what Lan thought, too?"

"No. My mother trusted you."

"I was on a clandestine mission to rescue POWs," he said. "I never intended to have an affair. But after I was injured, Lan sheltered me. She gave me food and medical care. And I—" His voice broke a little. "I didn't remember that I had a wife and children in America."

"My mother believed with all her heart that you were single."

"And so did I." He glanced at the windows, at the landscaped view of Crofthaven. "But I'm not sure why a married man would feel that way. Even a man with amnesia."

He frowned, and Lea wondered if he'd told his wife about his Vietnamese lover or if he'd kept his guilt bottled up inside. Either way, his marriage had suffered. Of that much, she was sure.

When Abraham sat next to her, Lea struggled to breathe. He was so close, she could see the tiny lines around eyes. She wanted to touch his face, to imagine him forgiving her, but she didn't dare.

"I cared very deeply for Lan," he said.

"Did you?" she asked, clasping her hands on her lap.

"Yes, very deeply. But after I was rescued and taken to a U.S. Naval hospital in Hawaii, I was told that Lan's village and all of its inhabitants were destroyed. Because of me," he added. "Because of the aid they'd given a U.S. soldier."

"My mother didn't die." Lea looked around for Michael and noticed that he remained standing, like a sentry, at the opposite end of the room. He caught her gaze and gave her a small nod of encouragement, letting her draw from his strength. "She lived for many years after that."

Her father sighed. "I wish I had known."

"Why?" she asked honestly. "What would you have done? Brought her to America once diplomatic relations with Vietnam were restored? Presented her to your wife and children?"

Abraham's response was troubled, as painful as

his solution. "I wouldn't have left her there. I wouldn't have betrayed her. Lan and her family risked their lives to keep me safe, to hide me from the Viet Cong."

"Yes, she told me that. She said her uncle was involved in the secret mission you were on. That he brought you to their village because you were badly injured and separated from your unit."

"He was injured, too. But he didn't survive his wounds." Although Abraham cleared his throat, he wasn't able to clear the discomfort from his voice. "Did Lan wait for me? Did she hope that I would come back for her someday?"

"Yes. And I hoped and prayed you would, too."

"Until you started hating me?"

Her stomach clenched. This was the man her mother had loved, the man who'd fueled Lea's childhood dreams, the flesh-and-blood hero she'd lost. "I'm so sorry I threatened you. I had no right to make you fearful. To force you to worry about your family."

"It's so hard to believe it was you."

She wanted to curl up and cry, but she knew it wouldn't lessen her crime. "You can contact the police. I'll understand if you turn me in."

Abraham sat quietly for a moment, contemplating her words; he glanced at Michael, then back at her. "I could never do that."

"Why not?" she asked.

"Because you're my daughter."

"But I lashed out at you. I didn't treat you like a father."

"You were hurting." He handed her the lemonade she'd yet to drink. "You're still hurting."

"And so are you." She could see how deeply Lady Savannah had affected him. "I don't deserve your compassion."

"But I want you to accept it. For yourself and your mother."

She sipped her drink, clutching the glass like a lifeline. Somewhere deep down, he was still angry with her, she thought. Still disappointed in Lan's child. But he was trying to do the right thing. "Thank you for your kindness."

He gave her a small smile. "Maybe you and I should get to know each other. Maybe we could spend some time together this week."

"I'd like that." She tried to keep her hands from trembling, her heart from spilling over with tears. "I'd like that very much."

# Nine

After Michael and Lea left Crofthaven, they went back to Michael's house. But they couldn't seem to think of anything to say. Neither of them had anticipated her father's forgiveness. Lea's encounter with Danforth had turned out differently than they'd assumed it would. Better, but far more emotional than either of them could endure.

Lea's eyes, he noticed, were damp with unshed tears. Happy tears, sad tears, tears of shame. Michael wasn't sure how to comfort her.

"I should pack," she said.

"Pack?" he parroted. They stood in the great room, beneath the skylight, just looking at each other.

"To go home. Back to my apartment."

"But you've only been here a week. I invited you to stay for two weeks."

"You brought me here because you were investigating me. And the investigation is over."

He couldn't deny her claim. He'd suggested that they become friends, but his offer was based on solving Lady Savannah's case. "I did what I had to do." But he didn't like feeling this distant, this disconnected from her. "It was part of my job."

"I know." She glanced up at the skylight. "I think my father accepted me so readily because of his guilt."

"Because he cheated on his wife? Because Lan's village was destroyed? Because she raised his child on her own?" Michael blew out a rough breath. "He has a lot to contend with."

"I shouldn't have threatened him." She turned toward the stairs. "I only made things more difficult."

"It's over now. And you're both trying to make amends." He followed her upstairs, but he didn't stop her from packing, from making the choice to leave.

She removed her suitcase from the closet and placed it on her side of the bed. He sat on the opposite end, watching her, thinking how fragile she looked.

"Do you think my father will introduce me to his other children?" she asked.

"I imagine he will. Maybe not right away, but eventually."

She began folding her clothes, stacking them neatly in the suitcase. "Once the pain lessens?"

"Yes." A strand of her hair fell forward and Michael imagined tucking it behind her ear, touching the side of her face, absorbing the warmth of her skin. "I have no idea how your brothers and sister will feel. Some of them are probably still struggling with their relationship with their dad."

She held a ruffled blouse against her chest, clinging to the feminine fabric. "What if I cause more trouble than I'm worth?"

"You won't." He resisted the urge to hold her, to wrap her in his arms, to ask her to stay. But he knew they needed some time away from each other, time to sort out their feelings, to cope with the lies and betrayal.

She placed the ruffled blouse in her suitcase, smoothing the lapels. "I couldn't bear to hurt my father again." She stopped packing, her voice laced with shame. "Do you how I located him to begin with?"

Michael studied her weary expression. "No. How?"

"By chance." She smoothed her errant hair. "When I first came to America, I was young and poor and naive. I had no idea how vast this country was or how difficult it would be to locate someone."

"So what did you do?"

"Not much, not when I first got here. I showed his picture around, but that got me nowhere." She made a sad sound. "Do you know how many Amerasians were doing that? Carting around old photographs of their fathers?"

"But you found your dad."

"Only because he was running for state senator. By that time, I was conducting Internet searches, using *Abraham* and *Vietnam veteran* as key words. And one day, an article about Abraham Danforth popped up. There was a picture of him when he was in his twenties, when he fought in the war." She stopped packing. "I recognized him instantly. I knew it was the same man."

Michael thought about the snapshot she'd been carrying around. "I don't understand why Danforth agreed to have his picture taken with your mother, especially after the fall of Saigon."

"He didn't agree to it. He didn't know he was being photographed."

"Who took the picture?"

"Trung, my mother's younger brother. He was an amateur photographer."

Which meant he'd developed it himself, Michael thought. "Why was Trung sneaking around? Taking risky pictures?"

"Because my mother asked him to. She wanted a tangible connection to my father, something to hold on to if he was captured or killed."

Michael shook his head. "That picture could have gotten *her* captured or killed."

"I know. But she promised her brother that she would keep it well hidden. That she wouldn't let the Viet Cong find it." Lea paused. "But her promise hardly mattered because everyone in her family died, including Trung. She was the only person in her village who managed to escape."

Michael pictured Lan running for her life, dodging bullets, grenades and mortar blasts, hiding in a makeshift shelter, alone and afraid. "Will you show me the photograph Trung took? I want to see what your mother looked like."

"It's at my apartment." Lea resumed packing, folding her clothes, gathering her toiletries, keeping her hands much too busy. "You can stop by sometime to see it." She glanced up, and suddenly their gazes locked, trapping him in a timeless moment.

If he stopped by to see the photograph, would he end up in her bed? Would he become her midnight lover again?

"It wouldn't be right," he said.

She blinked. "What?"

"Nothing. I was just thinking out loud." And wishing their relationship wasn't so forbidden, that his feelings for Lea weren't tied up in knots, that he wasn't missing her already.

Lea told herself she enjoyed living alone, but on Monday, after her workday ended, she wandered around her apartment as restless as a caged cat.

She changed into a halter dress, dusted her furniture, turned on the TV and switched channels a dozen times.

When the doorbell rang, she leaped off the couch, hoping it was Michael. She missed him terribly.

Anxious, she answered the summons and found Cindy on the other side. The blonde was dressed in a mint-colored suit, looking as cool and fresh as the icy green fabric. Somehow, the sweltering August weather didn't seem to have an effect on her.

"I hope you don't mind that I stopped by," Cindy said. "I got your address from your file at the office."

"Of course I don't mind." Lea wasn't sure what to make of this visit, but she invited the other woman inside.

"What a lovely apartment." Cindy looked around with unabashed curiosity. "Smart and tidy."

"Thank you. Would you like some iced tea? I always keep a fresh pitcher on hand."

"That sounds good." The blonde followed Lea to the kitchen, making herself at home. She sat at the glass-topped table near the window and crossed her legs.

Lea poured their drinks and joined her. "Did you come here directly from the office?"

"Yes. As a matter of fact, that's why I decided to stop by. Michael drove me crazy today." Cindy accepted the tea and took a small sip. "He was so moody." She leaned forward. "I assume you two are having some problems."

Lea didn't know what to say. She certainly couldn't tell Cindy that Michael had been investigating her. "I have a lot going on in my personal life."

"With what? Your father?"

"Yes. We're going to try to get to know each other."

"So you're ready to let him announce to the world that you're his daughter?"

"No. I mean...I think it's still too soon for that. I'd prefer to keep our relationship private for a while."

Cindy tilted her head. "I wonder if he'll include you in his will."

Taken aback, Lea could only stare. She hadn't expected the other woman to pry into Abraham's financial affairs, at least not in such a blatant manner. "I'm not interested in my father's money."

"Then what is it you want from him?"

"Acceptance." And forgiveness, she thought. Absolution. Redemption.

The blonde fluffed her hair, tossing loose waves over her shoulders. "I'd rather have his money. Let's face it, that man owes you. There you were, abandoned in Vietnam and struggling to get by while his other children were attending fancy boarding schools."

At this point, Lea wasn't sure if Cindy was friend or foe, enemy or ally. "I used to think that he owed me something, but I don't feel that way any more."

The other woman's tennis bracelet glinted in the light. "I didn't mean to speak ill of your father. Abraham Danforth is a fascinating man. A bit too old for my taste, but charming nonetheless."

Too old? Did that mean Cindy wasn't keeping a romantic eye on him?

"Now Michael is perfect, don't you think?"

Lea stumbled. "P-perfect? For what?"

"Someone our age." The bracelet caught another ray of light. "I'm twenty-seven. Just like you."

"I never considered Michael's age as a factor in our relationship."

"Didn't you? Well, think about it. A successful man in his midthirties is just what a career-oriented woman in her late-twenties needs."

When Lea didn't respond, they sat quietly, drinking sugar-spiked tea and listening to the background noise of the television, a talk show offering marital advice.

"I'll bet he's going to show up here," Cindy said.

"Who?"

"Michael."

"Why would he?"

"Because he was thinking about you all day. He didn't tell me he was, but he didn't have to. I know him better than anyone. I can read his moods." The other woman sighed. "I wish someone like Michael would brood over me."

Someone *like* Michael? Lea wondered. Or Michael himself? With Cindy, it was impossible to tell. The blonde never quite made her intentions clear.

Cindy leaned back in her chair. "It's a sexual obsession."

Lea's pulse jumped. "What?"

"The way Michael feels about you. I'll bet he'll ask you to move in with him. Just to have you next to him every night."

"He won't—"

"Yes, he will. That's what my old boyfriend did with me. And once the excitement wore off, he got rid of me." Cindy rose, leaving her half-empty glass on the table. "I should go. I have some errands to run."

Dazed, Lea could only stare.

With the grace of a Savannah socialite, Cindy reached out to give Lea a hug, confusing her even more. And by the time the blonde swept out the door in her mint-green attire and diamond trinkets, Lea's head was spinning.

Fifteen minutes later the doorbell sounded, but Lea wasn't surprised to find Michael waiting on her stoop. Cindy claimed that he would stop by, and she was right.

Michael gave Lea a cautious smile, and her heart melted. God, how she loved him.

"Should I have called first?" he asked.

"No. I'm glad you're here."

He entered the apartment, and they stood quietly for a moment, just looking at each other. He was dressed in a white shirt, black trousers and a silk tie, with his hair combed away from his forehead. She wanted to kiss him, to lead him to her room, but she couldn't bring herself to do that, not after what Cindy had said.

He lifted the grocery bag in his hand. "I got the ingredients for the pumpkin soup. I found a Seminole recipe online that's similar to what my mom used to make."

"Then come into the kitchen and we'll cook."

"Okay." He smiled at her again, leaving her breathless.

Lea cleared the iced-tea glasses from the table, and Michael set the groceries on the counter. When she turned to face him, he was removing his tie and rolling up his shirtsleeves.

She moved closer to unpack the ingredients, and he roamed his gaze over her.

"Is that a new dress?" he asked.

She nodded. "I bought it yesterday."

"It's backless." He tossed his tie over the back of a kitchen chair. "Braless."

Her nipples went hard. Guilty for wanting him, she fussed with her hair, bringing it forward, covering her breasts. "It's been so hot lately."

He jammed his hands into his pockets. "Do you think it's too hot to make soup?"

"In Vietnam, we used to have soup for breakfast. I can eat it anytime. In any kind of weather."

"Me, too." He unpacked the grocery bag. "The recipe calls for two cups of chicken stock, so I bought bouillon cubes. Is that okay?"

She still wanted to touch him, to lead him to her room, to hold him as close as she could. "Sure. That's fine."

"I got canned pumpkin. I didn't see any fresh pumpkins at the market." He handed her the recipe he'd printed from the Internet. "But supposedly either one works."

She glanced at the paper. "I'm sure it will be good."

"I hope so." He stepped forward, closing the gap between them. "I've missed you so much, Lea. It's only been two days, but I can hardly stand it."

When she looked up at him, the room nearly tilted. "I feel exactly the same way."

"I kept hoping you did." He brought her against his body, stroking a hand down her naked back, creating a blanket of warmth over her skin.

She put her head on his shoulder and inhaled the familiar scent of his cologne. He was everything she wanted, everything that mattered.

"We need to start over," he said. "A clean slate. No lies, no false pretenses. No Lady Savannah."

"I'm not her anymore." Lea lifted her head. "I swear, I'm not."

"I know. I trust you." He cupped her face. "We'll have a real relationship this time. Deeper than before."

Their conversation swirled around her like a soul-shrouding mist. Michael stood before her asking her to become a significant part of his life. Yet somewhere deep down, it didn't feel right.

Because of Cindy, she thought. Because the seed of doubt had already been planted. "It scares me."

He took his hand away. "Why?"

"It seems too good to be true."

"There's nothing that can spoil it this time. Move in with me, Lea. Share my house."

Her knees nearly buckled, Cindy's prediction reverberating in her ears. "Maybe we should date for a while first."

"Why? What's wrong with living together?"

"If it doesn't work out, I don't think I could survive. We've been through so much already." And she couldn't bear to think that his feelings for her were based on sex, on an obsession he couldn't control. "We shouldn't rush into this."

"Okay. Fine." He scooped her into his arms. "Then I'll court you. I'll wine and dine you. I'll do all those romantic things women want." He dragged her heart against his. "I'll make you swoon."

Her insides turned to mush. "You already have."

"Then I'm just going to keep doing it." He kissed her, deep and rich and slow.

He tasted like a forbidden dream, like the mysterious vampire from her past. His lips were smooth and moist, his chin bristling with a five o'clock shadow. She liked the raspy feeling, the slight roughness against her cheek.

By the time the kiss ended, her heart was reeling. She wondered if it would always be this way or if Michael would lose interest in her someday.

He touched a lock of her hair. "Can I see that picture of your parents?"

"Of course." She wanted to share it with him. She wanted him to know every part of her. "I'll get it."

She went into her bedroom and removed an envelope from her jewelry box. After she returned to the kitchen, she handed Michael a photograph ravaged by time and the remnants of war.

He studied it carefully. "Lan was beautiful. You look a lot like her."

"Thank you. My father was handsome, too." Abraham was young and tall and lean, a secret soldier recovering from his injuries.

"Have you heard from him?"

She nodded. "He called me at work today. He invited me to Crofthaven."

"When?"

"Tomorrow, before it gets dark. He wants to walk on the beach."

Michael returned the photograph. "That sounds nice. There's a private cove. I'm sure you'll enjoy it."

She tucked the picture into the envelope, closing the flap, preserving the only image she had of her mother. "I'm nervous about it."

"You'll be fine."

He reached out to hug her, to press a gentle kiss on her forehead, and she let herself fall deeper in love, no matter how dangerous it was.

A moment later, she told herself to take a cleansing breath, to live one day at a time, to cook the soup with Michael and fill her kitchen with the aroma of pumpkin, parsley, sugar and thyme.

# Ten

Seagulls flocked along the shore, and the sky reflected a prism of summer hues.

"This is beautiful," Lea said.

Her father guided her along the secluded beach, the sun-warmed sand glistening at their feet. "It's peaceful. A good place to be alone."

Lea nodded, then turned to look at him. His hair blew in the breeze, stirring lightly in the air. She wanted to apologize again, but she feared talking about Lady Savannah would break the spell.

Self-conscious, she smoothed her wind-ravaged T-shirt. She'd fussed over her appearance, worried that she would never be as pretty as his other daughter. Abraham had five legitimate children, four boys and a girl. Lea had seen newspaper pictures of them.

They were adults, like her, but as far as she knew, they'd never done anything as cold-hearted as threaten their father.

"Have you told your other children about me?" she asked.

"Yes, I have. I told them after I received the results from the paternity test."

"Were they upset?"

He stopped walking. "They were upset that I'd slept with another woman while I was married to their mother. But I think they're coming to terms with the amnesia."

She studied his frown. "Are you?"

"My marriage wasn't as strong as it should have been."

Because of his guilt? she wondered. Or because he wasn't a good husband to begin with?

"Do you want to meet your brothers and your sister?" he asked.

Lea took a deep breath. "Yes, very much." She looked into her father's eyes, hoping his other children were interested in her.

Abraham held her gaze. "Then I'll let them know and they can contact you when they're ready. I don't want to arrange a family dinner. I think it would be better to let everyone handle this in his or her own way."

"I understand. I think I'd prefer that, too. I'd be too nervous at a family dinner."

"It will get easier with time." He gave her a reassuring smile. "We're already making progress."

She returned his smile, knowing her mother

would be pleased. "I have something to show you." She reached into her backpack and removed the faded photograph, handing it to him.

He gazed at the black-and-white image of himself with Lan. "I didn't know someone took a picture of us." He handled the glossy paper carefully, his voice edged with emotion. "It must have been Trung."

"It was. But at my mother's request. She wanted a picture with you." Lea thought about the years her mother struggled to survive, the days she'd cried for her American lover. "She missed you."

"I'm sorry, Lea." He watched her hair blow across her face. "I'm so sorry."

"So am I." She stepped forward to take a chance, to embrace him. "For everything I've done."

He returned her hug, holding her tentatively at first, then stronger, smoothing her long, billowing hair. She closed her eyes for a moment, realizing her mother's picture was between them.

When they separated, her eyes turned misty.

"I'm still willing to call a press conference," he said. "To let the public know about you. To claim you as my daughter."

"That means the world to me, but I'm not ready to talk to reporters, to have them coming to my door. I'd prefer to remain in the background for a while."

"That's fine. I just wanted you to know the offer still stands."

He returned the photograph, and Lea decided her mother was right. Abraham Danforth was an honorable man.

* * *

John Van Gelder accepted a snifter of brandy from Hayden, giving his young adviser a wary look. At this point, John didn't know whom to trust. Honest Abe was leading in the polls, fooling the public into believing he was the candidate of choice. "This better be good."

"The brandy?"

"Your news."

"It is." Hayden leaned against the desk in his study, a bit too confident, too sure of himself.

He reminded John of a peacock fanning its feathers, but that wasn't enough to convince him that the boy had done his job. "What do you have? What did you find out?"

"Abraham Danforth took a paternity test last month."

John didn't react, not at first. "How accurate is this information?"

"My source is extremely reliable. The person I spoke with is absolutely certain that Danforth fathered an illegitimate child."

"Well, I'll be damned." A smile spread across John's face. "That is good news." He finished the brandy, savoring the feeling, the sudden flavor of success. He knew it wouldn't take long for Danforth's reputation to crumble, not once this juicy little tidbit was leaked to the press. "I believe we just caught Honest Abe with his pants down."

"Yes, sir," Hayden said, refilling John's glass. "I believe we did."

* * *

After Lea returned from the beach, she got ready for a date with Michael. He'd offered to take her to a popular nightspot, keeping his promise to wine and dine her. So she put on a short black dress and piled her hair loosely on top of her head, hoping to look chic and stylish.

At 9:00 p.m. they arrived at Steam, a trendy club and posh restaurant located downtown. Less than five minutes later, they were seated at one of the best tables in the house.

Intrigued, Lea glanced around. The dining room was located on the second floor, directly above the club. From her vantage point, she could see the stage below. Both the restaurant and club were decorated in red velvet, with touches of mahogany and marble.

"Clayton Crawford owns this place," Michael said. "He's a good friend of mine."

She reached for her menu. "No wonder we're getting the royal treatment."

"I told Clay about you. He knows about Lady Savannah, the whole bit. I had to confide in someone."

"He must think I'm awful."

"I let him know you were working things out with your dad."

She relaxed a little. The lamp on the table glowed, and their glasses were already filled with wine. "I assume I'll get to meet Clay tonight?"

"And his fiancée, too." He looked over the balcony. "They're down there somewhere. We can hook up with them later."

When their server came by, Lea and Michael ordered the same meal: a steak and seafood platter, with sautéed vegetables and Cajun spices.

"This is nice," she said.

He met her gaze. "It is, isn't it?"

"You know how to treat a woman right."

"You're the most important person in the world to me." His voice turned rough, laced with trepidation, with tenderness, with a jumble of emotions. "Am I that important to you?"

Her heart nearly quit beating, but that didn't stop her from reaching across the table for his hand, from admitting the truth. "I love you, Michael."

"Really?" Although he gripped her fingers like a vise, his voice still sounded rough, still edged with anxiety. "Then why won't you move in with me?"

"Because you're still struggling with your feelings."

He didn't dispute her claim. "Clay thinks I love you. He thinks I've got it bad."

And Cindy thinks it's about sex, Lea thought. So who was right?

When the server brought their bread, they separated, taking their hands back, leaving the table free.

"How do you know that you love me?" he asked suddenly.

"I just do." She wasn't sure how to explain her feelings, not to a man who was watching her with fear in his eyes. "It's okay if it scares you."

He picked up his wine. "All I ever think about is touching you. Putting my hands all over you." He leaned forward. "Is that what love is supposed to be like?"

"I don't know what it's like for men."

He frowned a little. "Neither do I." He finished his drink, then poured another glass. "Maybe we should stop talking about it."

Lea agreed, so they sat quietly, sipping chardonnay and buttering warm bread. When their meal arrived, they ate filet mignon and grilled shrimp, catching anxiety-ridden glimpses of each other between bites.

Halfway through their food, Michael started another conversation. "I'm going to be the best man at Clay's wedding."

She tasted her vegetables. "When is it?"

"Near the end of the month. Do you want to go with me?"

"Yes. I'd like that very much."

"Good." He smiled at her. "I want this to work, Lea. I want us to make it."

"Me, too." She looked into his eyes and saw her own dreams, the wishes of a *con lai* girl who'd fallen in love with a half-breed boy.

After dinner, they took a gated elevator to the lower level, and once they were in the club, he introduced her to Clay Crawford and his fiancée, a stunning redhead named Kat.

Lea couldn't help but admire them, the soul-stirring way they looked at each other, the tender yet subtle way they touched.

Clay seemed to be watching her and Michael, too, analyzing them, judging their relationship. But Lea didn't mind. If the other man thought that Michael loved her, then she was more than willing to consider him an ally.

Within a few minutes, Clay and Kat excused themselves, insisting they had work to do. But Lea wasn't buying their excuse. She suspected that they wanted to give her and Michael some romantic time alone.

Once his friends were gone, Michael gazed at her. She looked back at him, wishing she could lock him inside her heart.

"Do you want to dance?" he asked.

She nodded and reached for his hand. Together, they walked onto the dance floor, finding a cozy spot among the other couples.

The music was deep and sensual, as rhythmic as the motion of their bodies. He lowered his head to kiss her, and she tasted the wine he'd drunk with dinner, the flavor of intoxication on his lips. Lea had never danced like this before. She'd never moved so erotically, not with her clothes on.

He nuzzled her neck, breathing softly against her skin, and when he loosened the pins in her hair, she wondered if he knew he was seducing her.

"Will you stay with me tonight?" she asked, not wanting to be alone, to be without him.

"You know I will." He kissed her again, and at that desperate moment, Lea told herself it didn't matter if Michael knew the difference between lust and love. All that mattered was his hands and his mouth and the slow, sensual way he caressed her.

Yes, she thought. All that mattered was the beauty of making love with him, the comfort of his touch, the sweet, summer-bound safety of sleeping in his arms.

\* \* \*

Michael awakened in Lea's bed, in a room with lavender sheets and whitewashed furniture.

Feeling out of place in the feminine surroundings, he tried to acclimate his emotions, the fear of falling in love, of being overwhelmed by it, of not knowing which way to turn or what to do.

Confused, he breathed against her neck, inhaling the familiar scent of her skin. She was still asleep, still wrapped in his arms.

He disengaged their bodies and rose on his elbow, leaning over her. She squinted and opened her eyes, fluttering her lashes, fighting grogginess.

"What are you doing?" she asked.

He managed a smile. They'd made sweet, syrupy love last night, touching and kissing for hours, making every breathless minute count. "I'm looking at you."

"Why?"

"Because you're so pretty." And because when he was with her, when she was by his side, his life made sense. And when she wasn't, he went crazy. "I wish you'd move in with me."

She reached out to graze his cheek. "We agreed to take our time about that."

Michael frowned. In some ways, he understood her reluctance. And in other ways, it made him ache. "You think I'm being impulsive."

"You are." She traced the troubled lines in his forehead. "But I'm still in love with you."

He lowered his head to kiss her, wishing he had more control over what was happening. The only time their relationship seemed stable was when he was inside her, when their bodies were joined, when they got lost in each other's arms.

She slid her hands through his hair, pulling him closer. They were still naked, still warm and sticky from the night before.

"I don't have any more condoms with me," he said.

"It's okay. We don't have to be together."

"But I want to make you feel good." Unable to resist, he rubbed his thumbs over her nipples, making them peak, drawing one into his mouth.

Lea arched and sighed, and he took comfort in the closeness, in the intimacy that never failed to arouse her. Anxious to please her, he roamed her body, molding her, taking possession.

She gave him a glazed look, and he knew she'd slipped into a state of carnal consciousness, that his soul was seeping into her pores.

"I can't concentrate when you touch me," she said. "I can't think clearly."

"Good." He didn't want her to behave rationally. He wanted her to come unglued, to surrender to him. "Do you like this?" He licked his way to her navel. "And this?" He nipped her skin, moving lower, making her moan.

When she opened her legs, inviting him to taste her, he kissed between her thighs, using his tongue, giving her what she wanted, what they both needed.

Heat, he thought. Primal sensations. Sleek, seductive shivers.

She made a throaty sound, and sunlight spilled

into the room, bathing her in ever-changing hues, in colors his mind had conjured.

Lea wasn't shy. She lifted her hips and rubbed against his mouth, showing him how much she liked what he was doing.

He liked it, too. For Michael, oral sex was more than foreplay, more than a teasing game. To him, it was the ultimate act of submission, of trusting your partner.

When she climaxed, he tasted her release, sipping her deep and slow. She fell onto the bed, her stomach muscles quivering, her limbs shaking.

He'd never seen a more beautiful woman.

"You're spoiling me," she said.

He kissed his way back up her body, brushing her lips with his. "That's the idea."

She rolled over. "Maybe I should spoil you."

His pulse pounded. Everywhere. "You don't have to."

"What if I want to?" She crawled between his thighs, making his breath catch. He was already hard, already turned on.

Michael shifted his legs, giving her full access to his body, letting her have as much as she wanted, as much as she was willing to take.

She took all of him, with her hands and her mouth, increasing the tempo, setting a strong, fluid rhythm.

Mesmerized, he toyed with her hair, twining it around his fingers, making the moment even more erotic. Falling deeper under her spell, he yielded to the pressure in his loins, to the warmth and the wetness.

He knew he should warn her that he was getting close, that he was on the verge of losing control, but he couldn't summon the strength to give up the pleasure, to lessen the mind-blowing gratification. So he watched her instead, getting more and more turned on.

Time passed, seconds, minutes. He didn't care. He couldn't think beyond the sucking motion, beyond the way she made him feel.

She gave him everything—every raw, ravenous sensation a man could imagine, every hot wicked thing he could fantasize about.

Michael cupped her face, knowing he was going to spill into her, knowing she was going to let him.

After it was over, they stared at each other, stunned, confused, strangely aroused. He wasn't sure if he should apologize or drag her against his body and kiss her senseless.

He did neither. He simply accepted their newfound intimacy, curious when she ran her tongue across her lips.

"Salty?" he asked.

She nodded, then reached for the bottled water beside her bed and took a sip. "I've never gone that far before."

His skin turned warm. "Me, neither." He'd always pulled back before he climaxed, never expecting any of his lovers to do what Lea had just done. "What an incredible way to start the day."

"For you," she said, making a face.

He laughed, and she splashed him, spraying his chest. He grabbed her, and they tumbled over the sheets, wresting with the plastic bottle and dumping the rest of the water onto the bed.

And at that silly, lighthearted moment, he prayed that he would never lose her, that she was his to keep.

His cell phone rang, interrupting their horseplay, jarring his tender thoughts. Cursing his job, he answered it, sensing it was a business call.

"Michael?" Cindy's frantic voice came on the line. "Have you seen the paper this morning?"

"No. I'm at Lea's. What's going on?"

"It made the front page."

"What did?" he asked, although he was already gathering his clothes, already preparing to get dressed. Cindy wasn't the type to overreact.

"The paternity test. Someone leaked it to the press."

He glanced at his lover, cursing out loud this time. "Does the article mention Lea?"

"No. It's speculation, mostly. But it doesn't look good for Mr. Danforth."

He yanked up his pants. "Lea and I will meet you at the office. Send the rest of the team to Crofthaven."

"I already did."

"Good. We'll see you soon." He hung up and told Lea to get ready, knowing all hell was about to break loose.

# Eleven

Lea sat at a long wooden table in a meeting room at Whittaker and Associates, with the newspaper strewn in front of her. She'd barely had time to catch her breath and now her stomach was burning from drinking the coffee Cindy had poured into her cup. She still hadn't told the other woman she preferred tea, and Michael was too preoccupied to notice.

"I feel so responsible," Cindy said. She walked around to the other side of the table, moving closer to Michael. "It was my job to make sure this didn't happen." She took the chair next to him. "Maybe it was someone at the lab."

"Or someone who works for Danforth's attorneys." He smoothed his sleep-tousled hair. "There are only a handful of people who knew about the test. And this is only going to get worse."

Cindy agreed. "The tabloids are going to have a field day. They'll probably link Mr. Danforth with every socialite in Savannah. Married, single. Anyone with a young child."

Silent, Lea glanced at the article about her father. The press didn't know he'd fathered a grown daughter. And being omitted from the scandal made her feel like a cheat, like she'd skimmed by purposely, allowing her dad to take the fall.

Michael blew out a frustrated breath. "Being a political figure isn't easy. The press plays a dirty game."

"They sure do," the blonde said.

Once again, guilt clawed at Lea's conscience. Hoping to settle her stomach, she reached for a croissant and took a small bite. Cindy had provided a variety of baked goods, something, Lea assumed, the blonde did for her boss every morning.

He decided to eat, too, spreading cream cheese onto a bagel. He didn't look like a man who'd spent the last hour engaging in erotic acts with his lover. He was all business now, except for his wrinkled clothes, the same shirt and trousers he'd worn to the club the night before.

Lea wasn't faring much better. She'd grabbed a T-shirt and jeans, barely having time to wash her face and brush her teeth. Cindy, of course, looked as polished as a new penny. Everything about her shimmered, including the copper-colored buttons on her designer suit.

"How's it going at Crofthaven?" Michael asked his assistant.

"Our team is keeping the media circus away," she responded.

Lea finally spoke up. "I'm the one who's responsible for this mess. If I had agreed to a press conference with my father, none of this would have happened." She reached for the paper. "Is it too late to do it now?"

Michael glanced up at her, ignoring his half-eaten bagel. She caught Cindy's attention, as well.

"It's not too late," he said. "But it won't be easy on you. The press will want to delve into every aspect of your life."

She put on a brave face. "I owe this to my father."

Cindy chimed in. "I think it's the perfect solution, Michael. If Mr. Danforth and his Amerasian daughter show a united front, it will create a positive image for both of them." She turned to Lea. "And there's nothing in your past that won't endear you to the public."

Except Lady Savannah, she thought. And that was a private matter, between her and her father.

"Are you sure you're ready to do this?" Michael asked.

"Yes, I'm sure." What choice did she have? She couldn't let her dad suffer. She couldn't allow the media to make up stories about him, pairing him with half the women in Savannah, gossiping, speculating about who had given birth to his child.

Michael leaned forward. "I'll call your father and

let him discuss this with his campaign manager. They can arrange the press conference." He snared her gaze. "It would probably be better if you moved in with me, at least for a while. My house is secure. The paparazzi can't bother you there."

"I'll be okay." She didn't want to use this as an excuse to live with him. She wanted to be sure he loved her first, that he wasn't confused about his feelings.

"Fine. I'll make that call from my office." He stood, taking his coffee with him. "I'll be back in a few minutes."

After he left the room, Cindy picked up a blueberry muffin. "You wounded his pride."

"I know." And now she feared she might lose him. "But what else could I do?"

"Nothing. You made the right decision."

"Did I?" She gazed at the other woman, a sudden chill icing her spine. A warning, she thought. But hadn't there been warning signs all along? "Who's the man you're interested in?"

Cindy lifted her chin. "Who do you think he is?"

"Michael," she said, her pulse pounding in her ears.

His assistant remained calm, poised as ever. "That's crazy." She picked at her muffin, taking delicate bites. "If I didn't know better, I'd think you were a suspicious shrew."

Lea narrowed her eyes. "Oh, really?"

"Yes, but you're not. You're just insecure."

"Why? Because you've convinced me not to move in with the man I love?"

"Living with Michael won't make him feel the same way about you. It will only give him what he wants." Cindy dusted the crumbs from her fingers. "A bedmate, someone to satisfy his needs. And you'll end up getting hurt."

Lea pushed away her croissant. She was already hurting, already fighting her fears.

A moment later, Michael came back, ready to resume their meeting. Both women turned to look at him, but neither of them breathed a word of the conversation they'd just had.

The press conference was being held at the Twin Oaks Hotel, the same location as the July Fourth fund-raiser where Lea had first confronted her father. For now, she waited in a hospitality suite, where Nicola Granville, Abraham's campaign manager and image consultant, had been giving her one last briefing, one last boost of encouragement.

Nicola was outgoing and confident, as well as smart and pretty. Lea had no idea if the other woman was involved with her father, but she recalled Michael's observation, his gut instinct that Abraham and Nicola were attracted to each other.

Nicola glanced at her watch. "I'm going to head over to the conference room to check on some details. Just relax, Lea. And I'll come back for you when it's time."

"Is my father here yet?"

"No, but he should be arriving shortly."

"Okay. Thanks." She reached for the root beer she'd been nursing. Michael was already at the conference room, but he'd stationed a bodyguard outside the hospitality suite in case anyone bothered Lea.

Nicola exited the room, leaving her alone with her thoughts. She had no idea where Cindy was today, but she was glad the deceptive blonde wasn't hovering nearby, making her more nervous than she already was. Although she intended to talk to Michael about his assistant, she wanted to wait until the press conference was over, until she could think clearly.

The bodyguard knocked on the door, then poked his head inside. "Two of your brothers are here to see you, Miss Nguyen."

"My brothers?" Lea hopped up from the couch, nearly spilling her drink. "Are you sure?"

"Yes, ma'am. I verified their identification. Adam and Marcus Danforth."

"Then send them in." She smoothed her dress, praying that she met with their approval.

A second later, when her brothers entered the room, Lea forgot to breathe. They looked more handsome in person than they did in the photographs she'd seen. Taller, broader, chiseled and strong.

"I'm Adam." The older of the two stepped forward. She knew his age—twenty-nine—because she'd memorized details about her siblings, things she'd read in newspaper and magazine clippings.

"I'm Lea." She smiled, and the greeting turned warm. Adam gave her a quick brotherly hug, and she sensed that was his way of welcoming her into the family.

"I don't suppose this is much fun," he said. "The press conference and all that."

"I'm nervous," she admitted, studying the hazel-gold color of his eyes. She'd come across some old tabloid articles about Adam, claiming that he'd been involved in a love triangle. Were the allegations true? She had no idea. But either way, he seemed to empathize with her situation.

Finally, her other brother moved forward. His eyes caught hers, and they gazed at each other. She knew he was a Harvard-educated lawyer, an attorney for Danforth and Company.

"You're Marcus," she said.

"Call me Marc."

Once again, they simply looked at each other. She couldn't explain the instant bond, the feeling that she trusted him already.

"I'm sorry about your mother, Lea. That you lost her before you came to America."

"Thank you." She hadn't expected any of Abraham's children to mention his Vietnamese lover. She'd assumed Lan would be a taboo subject, someone they would prefer to sweep under the rug if they could. "I'm sorry you lost your mother, too."

"It was a long time ago," he said. "I was just a kid."

But it hadn't been easy on him, she thought. "I'm so glad you and Adam stopped by. This means so much to me."

"You're our new sister." Marc glanced at his brother. "We've always been loyal. To each other," he added, indicating that their father hadn't always garnered their loyalty, that his absence, the years he'd spent on his military career, had created a void in their lives. "Ian, Reid and Kim couldn't make it today. But I'm sure you'll be hearing from them before long."

Overwhelmed, she blinked back tears. "I'm looking forward to meeting my other brothers, and of course my sister, too." She paused to take a much-needed breath. "I was worried about how she would feel about me."

Adam spoke up. "Kim should enjoy having another female around." He laughed a little. "Not that she didn't learn to hold her own around all of us."

Lea smiled, then realized she'd forgotten her manners. "Would either of you like a drink?" She gestured to the wet bar. "Nicola said it was stocked."

Her brothers declined the offer, admitting that they would prefer to skip out before their dad arrived. "It'll be easier if it's just the two of you at the press conference," Marc said, sounding like the attorney he was. "And Adam would just as soon avoid the limelight. Wouldn't you, bro?"

"You got that right." Adam reached for Lea's hand to say goodbye, wishing her luck. Marc said goodbye, too, giving her a hug this time, making her feel warm and protected.

After they left, she resumed her spot on the couch and waited for her father, for the man who'd given her a family.

When the press conference ended, Michael invited Lea to his house for dinner. After a day filled with public scrutiny, he wanted her to enjoy a quiet evening in a secluded location.

He turned to look at her. She seemed preoccupied, as though her thoughts kept drifting. While he mashed potatoes, she panfried pork chops and made gravy, but they hadn't talked about anything other than the meal.

"Are these too lumpy?" he asked.

She came over to him and checked the potatoes. "It depends on how you like them."

"It doesn't matter."

"Then go ahead and add a little milk."

"How much is a little?"

"This much." She poured the milk for him, and he took the opportunity to move closer to her.

"It went well today," he said, watching her, pretending to be focused on the potatoes.

"Yes, it did, considering the circumstances. It wasn't easy for my father to admit to the press that he'd committed adultery, even if his amnesia was to blame."

"He's been willing to do that since he met you."

"I know, but I still think it took a lot of courage on his part."

Michael took back the bowl, even though she'd finished mashing the potatoes for him. "The reporters are going to verify his story. They're going to research his medical records to make sure it's true."

"It doesn't matter." She turned down the flame on the stove, then covered the pork chops. "He doesn't have anything to hide. Not like me."

"The press isn't going to find out about Lady Savannah, Lea. That's not going to make the papers."

"No, but our affair probably will."

"I don't care if they figure out that we're sleeping together." He tried to search her gaze, wishing she would look at him. "Do you?"

"No." She fussed with the salad, adding a layer of grated cheese on top. "We don't have anything to be ashamed of."

Then why was she behaving so awkwardly? Perplexed, he leaned against the counter. "Are you okay? You seem sort of distant."

She finally glanced up. "I do have something on my mind."

"What?"

"Arranging some vacation time at work. I don't think I can handle being in the public eye right now."

"That's understandable." His heart began to pound, reminding him of the effect she had on him, of his need to be close to her. "Did you change your mind about staying here, too?"

"Yes, but just for a few days, just until the media attention dies down." She set the salad aside. Behind her, the pork chops sizzled, sending a mouthwatering aroma into the air. "You don't mind, do you?"

"Of course not. I offered to let you stay here." He moved to stand beside her, to brush her shoulder with his. "I'll take some time off, too. We can lounge around together."

She sent him a gracious smile. "Thank you. I really need your support right now."

He sensed that she had more on her mind. That she hadn't told him everything. But he decided to drop the subject until she had a chance to relax.

"I'm investigating the paternity test leak," he said, letting her know he intended to find out who'd created this mess.

"Really? Do you have any leads?"

"Not yet. But there are only a couple of avenues to follow. Only a few sources who knew about the test."

She stirred the gravy. "I'm sure you'll find out."

"I hope so." He liked the way she looked in his kitchen, creating a domestic atmosphere, making him feel warm and homey. "I'm certainly going to do my best."

A short while later, they dined by candlelight, with music playing on the stereo. Over dinner, she talked about her brothers and how happy she was that they'd made an effort to see her. Michael smiled, pleased Adam and Marc had endeared themselves to her.

After their meal ended, he suggested dessert on the patio. She agreed, and they sat outside, listening to the sounds of summer and eating chocolate ice cream.

The air was mild, the sky dotted with stars. In the distance, he could see his private dock and a boat he sometimes used on security detail.

Silent, he turned to study Lea. She still had on the

same clothes she'd worn to the press conference, and her hair was loose, falling to her waist like rain.

"Tell me what's going on," he said. "Besides your concern about being in the public eye."

She took an audible breath. "I'm having some problems with Cindy."

Concerned, he leaned forward in his chair. "What kind of problems?"

Lea stirred her ice cream. "I think she's trying to come between us."

Stunned, Michael could only stare. "Why would she do that?"

Her eyes locked onto his. "Because she's interested in you. You're the mystery man she's been pursuing."

"Did she tell you that?"

"No. She denied it, but I can tell it's true."

He shook his head, wondering what the hell was going on. He'd never expected a conversation like this to evolve, not with Lea. "Give me the facts, support your claim."

Her voice quavered a little. "She keeps telling me that your attraction to me is purely sexual. That it will never be anything more than that." Her eyes were still magnetized to his. "She says I'll end up getting hurt."

"And this is coming from a woman who's supposedly interested in me?" He set his bowl on the patio table. His appetite was gone, his stomach muscles tense. "Come on, Lea. Why would she want me if she thinks I'm such a dog?"

"Maybe she thinks you'd develop a deeper relationship with her. Or maybe she doesn't care, as long as you're rich. But either way, she's trying to drive us apart."

"You must have misunderstood her intentions. Cindy has been my assistant for nearly three years, and she's never come on to me. There's never been anything between us. It just isn't there."

"You hired her because of the way she looks. You even admitted that you like being around beautiful women." She lifted her chin. "You said that when we were at the gallery downtown, the first time I met her."

"I remember where we were and what I said." He struggled to hold his temper, to keep this discussion grounded. "But you're taking my statement out of context. I hired Cindy because she's competent. Her appearance was secondary."

Lea shoved her ice cream bowl next to his. "That's like saying men buy *Playboy* for the articles."

"What the hell is that supposed to mean? That's she's only pretending to be competent, and I'm too busy drooling over her to notice?" He resisted the urge to kick the rail of an empty chair. Already he was reliving the arguments his parents used to have. This was too damn close to the accusations his mom used to make, even when his dad wasn't screwing around. "There's nothing going on but your overactive imagination."

She heaved a labored breath, and his heart twisted in his chest. Didn't Lea realize how much she meant to him? Didn't she know how often he'd suffered because of her? How much he ached? How confused he was?

"My feelings for you aren't based on sex," he said, defending his jumbled emotions.

"Maybe not." She wrapped her arms around her middle. "But your feelings aren't based on trust, either."

He didn't respond. He couldn't think of an appropriate answer, not while his parents' screaming matches were spinning in his head. The anger. The jealousy. The infidelity. He'd sworn that he'd never let anything like that taint his life.

Lea came to her feet. She did her best to remain strong, to keep her legs steady, but he could see that she was starting to shake.

"You're playing right into Cindy's hands," she said. "And before long, she'll console you right into her bed."

"I'm not interested in my assistant. And she's not interested in me. Why can't you see that?" He stood, too. He towered over her by nearly a foot, and he wished she didn't look so delicate, so soft and pretty. "Cindy has been a model employee. As loyal as they come. Granted, she's shrewd. Tough, a little ruthless. But that's her business side."

"It's her personal side, too."

"I know she intimidates you, Lea. I noticed it from the beginning."

"And so did she. That's how she managed to get away with this. She probably wants us to argue about her, hoping you'll defend her."

"I can't condemn her, not without proof."

"I should be your proof. My instincts should be

enough. A woman knows when another woman is after her man."

"What about my instincts?" he snapped. "I'm the detective." And he knew jealousy could get out of hand, whether or not it was warranted.

Lea didn't respond. She turned and walked into the house, leaving him alone.

He cursed under his breath and followed her. "What are you doing?" he asked as she retrieved her purse.

She spun around to face him. "Did you expect me to stay here now?"

He struggled with his feelings, with letting her go, with losing her. "There's probably paparazzi camped outside your apartment."

She ignored his comment and moved toward the front door. "I'd fight for you if I could, if it would do any good. But how can I wage a war with Cindy when you're taking her side?" She looked into his eyes. "How can I have a future with a man who doesn't trust me?"

When she was gone, he realized she was right. He hadn't given her a chance. And that scared him as much as falling in love with her.

Nearly two hours later, Michael checked his watch. Anxious, he studied the Swiss timepiece, watching the second hand make another gut-wrenching sweep. He hadn't been able to get in touch with Lea. He'd been calling her house, but the answering machine kept picking up. How many messages could he leave?

He reached for the cordless phone again, only this time he dialed Abraham Danforth's private number.

The older man answered on the fourth ring. "Hello?"

"Evening, sir, it's Michael."

For a moment, silence met him on the other line. Then, "Are you calling for Lea?"

His pulse spiked. "Is she there?"

"Yes, but I can't promise that she'll speak with you. You hurt her, Michael."

"I know. I'm sorry. Things are just so messed up." He pulled a hand through his hair. "I'm messed up."

"You've been drinking?"

He glanced at the bottle on the end table. "Yes. I mean, no, not really. I've had a couple beers. Will you ask Lea if she'll talk to me?"

"Hold on, and I'll check."

"Thank you." Michael grabbed the beer and took it into the kitchen, pouring the rest of it down the sink. He wouldn't mind getting drunk, blurring his senses with a desperate buzz, but he knew it wouldn't help his cause.

Whatever the hell his cause was.

Danforth finally returned, jarring his thoughts, making him take a quick, choppy breath.

"I'll transfer your call to Lea's room," the former Navy SEAL commander said. "But if you upset her again, you'll be answering to me."

"I understand." Michael wasn't about to get cocky with her father. He'd created enough trouble for one night.

While he waited for Lea, he walked outside for

some air. The dessert bowls were still on the patio table, left over from their meal.

"Michael?" She came on the line. "My father said you wanted to talk to me."

He sat at the table. "I just wanted to know if you were okay. I've been leaving messages at your apartment."

"I went by there, but I saw some reporters, so I drove to Crofthaven instead."

"And your dad invited you to stay at the mansion?"

"Yes. I'm in one of the guest rooms."

He pictured her among the finery, sitting on a Chippendale bed, with a satin quilt and gold-tasseled pillows. "I'm glad you're with your family."

"Me, too."

He stared at the bowl in front of him, then recalled the way his mom used to break their dime-store dishes, smashing them after her husband had stormed out the door. "This reminds me of my parents."

"What does?"

"You, me. This thing with Cindy."

She sighed into the receiver. "Then you should understand how I feel."

"My dad couldn't even talk to a woman without my mom getting jealous."

"I'm not jealous of Cindy."

"You don't trust her." And that made him feel as though Lea didn't trust him, either.

Her voice turned sharp. "She did all of this on purpose, and you don't believe me."

He held his temper, knowing it wouldn't do any good to rehash the same argument. "If Cindy is as devious as you claim she is, then I've been tricked by two women. First by Lady Savannah and now my assistant."

"Lady Savannah only foiled you for a little while. Then you trapped her. You caught her at her own game."

Meaning what? That he was supposed to trap Cindy, too? What if he couldn't uncover any proof? What if there was nothing concrete, nothing but Lea's word against Cindy's? "I'm not going to the office for a few days. I don't want to deal with this until I've had some time off." He squeezed his eyes shut. "My nerves are shot. They're ripped to the bone."

"So are mine."

He opened his eyes. "I never meant to hurt you."

"But you did."

Yes, he'd hurt her. But he wasn't convinced that she hadn't just misunderstood Cindy, that she wasn't blowing everything out of proportion. "I need some time to think this through."

"I'm not stopping you, Michael."

"I know." He adjusted the phone, cradling it closer to his ear. She sounded distant, like she was fading from his life already. "Do you believe what I said earlier?"

She released an audible breath. "About what?"

"Our relationship. That my feelings for you aren't based on sex."

"I don't know. I'm not sure. It started off being about sex. We slept together on the first night we met."

"It's more than that now."

"Is it?"

"Yes." It was about what they'd confided in each other, the hours they'd spent talking, the moments they'd laughed, the comfort of holding her in his arms, of watching her sleep. "It's our friendship. The closeness we share."

"But we're losing that. It's going away."

Because the trust they'd built was shattering, he thought. Because another woman had come between them.

"I should go," she told him, her tone still distant, still faraway. "It's been a long day, and I'm tired."

He glanced up at the sky, at the shallow light from a three-quarter moon. "I guess it is getting late." And they'd run out of things to say, their conversation dissolving into the night.

# Twelve

The following week, Michael stared at the wall in front of him, wishing he could bang his head against it. He'd screwed up and now he was faced with the consequences.

Seated at the desk in his office, he dialed Cindy's extension. His assistant picked up, and her voice scraped his spine like tree-sharpened talons, like claws gouging his skin.

"I need to talk to you," he said.

"Just give me a second, and I'll be right there."

He tensed his jaw, hating himself for what he'd done. He'd broken Lea's heart and destroyed his own. He'd ruined what they had together, and now he missed her so much, he could barely breathe.

Cindy entered his office with a concerned expression. "Is there a problem?"

He gestured for her to sit. She took the leather chair in front of his desk and crossed her legs. Her skirt rode a little higher than usual, revealing too much thigh.

"I wonder what Lea would think of your outfit," he said.

She tilted her head. "We're not going to discuss that business with her again, are we?"

He raised his eyebrows. Three days ago, he'd confronted Cindy about Lea's accusations and she'd adamantly denied any wrongdoing. She'd even phoned Lea to apologize, but Lea had refused to take the call. "So you're sticking by your story?"

"It's not a story. I already explained why I said those things to your girlfriend."

He kept his gaze fixed on hers. "Because you were only trying to be her friend? Hoping to stop her from getting hurt?"

"That's right, but she twisted my good intentions." Cindy made a sympathetic sound. "Have you seen her? Spoken with her?"

"Not since she spurned your apology. And quite frankly, I don't blame her."

"I see." She shifted her legs, drawing her skirt up a little farther. "Are you angry that I told her that I thought you were using her? I'm sorry, Michael. But Lea is terribly insecure, and you're incredibly aggressive. Too powerful for her."

"Aggressive? Powerful? You mean ruthless, don't you?"

"Yes, I suppose so. But I'm the same way. You and I are cut from the same cloth."

"Which means what?" He reached for a loose paper clip on his desk. "That you and I would make a good team?"

She tucked her hair behind her ear, where a diamond hoop sparkled. "We already make a good team. We work well together."

He twisted the paper clip, bending its perfect shape. "That's what I used to think."

She tilted her head. "Used to? What's going on? Why are you treating me this way?"

"Cut the crap, Cindy. I'm not falling for your innocent routine this time." And it shamed him that he'd taken her word over Lea's, that he'd believed his backstabbing assistant and all of her carefully conceived lies. "I've been investigating the paternity test leak, and guess where all of the clues lead?"

She didn't respond. She simply waited for him to continue, her legs still crossed, her head still tilted.

"To this office," he said. "To you."

She barely flinched, barely batted an eyelash. "Do you have proof beyond a reasonable doubt?"

"I'm still working on the proof, but there's no reasonable doubt in my mind. You had the opportunity and the motive."

"What motive?" She squared her shoulders, giving him a cool, calculated look, showing him how ruthless she really was. "That squinty-eyed lover of yours?"

He pressed his palms on the desk, leaning forward, fighting the urge to clench his fists. "If you were a man, I'd deck you. I'd beat the living crap out of you."

"But I'm not a man, am I?" She came to her feet, smoothing her blouse, refusing to let him ruffle her feathers. "And there's no way you'll ever prove it was me who leaked that information. All you have is a few measly clues."

She was right. His chances of securing physical evidence were slim to none. But her poison-tipped reaction was enough. It was all he needed to end her sick game. "I want you out of here. Today. Now."

"That's fine by me. I'll find a better job." She fluffed her hair. "Even without a recommendation from you."

"Go clear your desk."

She shrugged, telling him in no uncertain terms that she would take as much time as she needed to gather her belongings.

When she walked out of his office, he picked up the phone, praying that Lea would forgive him.

Lea arrived at Whittaker and Associates. Filled with trepidation, she entered the building, preparing herself for another bout of pain.

And then she saw Michael.

He leaned against the reception desk, wearing a black suit, a white shirt and a narrow tie. A strand of his hair fell across his forehead, but it was the only thing out of place. He looked tall and strong and composed.

She glanced around the room, catching glimpses of leather and chrome. The building seemed vacant, almost hollow. Or maybe it was her emotions, the emptiness inside her. "Are you the only person here?"

He shook his head. "Cindy is in her office."

She steeled her gaze. "Then why did you ask me to come here?"

"So you could watch her walk out the door. She's packing, Lea. I fired her."

To keep herself from reacting too strongly, she headed over to the sofa and sat down, waiting to hear what else he had to say. He raked his hand through his hair, messing it up a bit more, and she realized he wasn't as collected as he appeared.

"Was it difficult for you to fire her?"

"Not in the least." He sat on the sofa, too. "But this is difficult. Looking at you, knowing you probably hate me."

"I never said I hated you."

He nearly ransacked her gaze, his eyes much too intense. "Does that mean you still love me?"

She took a deep breath, trying to stabilize her pulse, the jittery sensation in her veins. "I never stopped loving you, Michael."

He managed to smile. "I kept hoping you'd say that." His smile fell. "I'm so sorry that I didn't believe what you said about Cindy."

Lea glanced at the door that led to the offices. It was closed, tight and secure. "Did she do something to make you change your mind? Did she come on to you?"

"Yes, she did something." He removed his jacket, placing it on the arm of the sofa. "She didn't come on to me, but I discovered that she leaked the paternity test."

Weary, Lea clasped her hands on her lap. "So you fired her for a security breach?"

"It's not as simple as that."

"Why? Because she managed to break us up? Because you didn't see through her?"

"Yes." Sunlight spilled into the room, mocking his features, intensifying the discomfort he couldn't hide. "All the signs were there, but I wasn't thinking straight. Cindy started asking me for advice about this mystery man around the time I met you. But I was too absorbed in our affair to realize that she was talking about me. You were all I thought about. You were all that mattered." He paused, his voice rough. "You were on my mind before I opened my eyes in the morning, while I was at work, after I came home, when I went to sleep at night. You were always there."

"Me and Lady Savannah."

He reached for her hair, letting the dark strands slip through his fingers. "I thought about you more than Lady Savannah. Until I suspected the truth. Then both of you became my obsession."

She wanted to touch him, too. But she didn't dare, not now, not while her heart was pounding anxiously against her breast. "Why did you trust Cindy so much?"

"Because she never gave me any reason to doubt her in the past. She seemed tough and intuitive, like me. And I thought those qualities made her a good assistant."

Her stomach clenched, recalling how many times

the other woman had predicted what Michael would do. "She said she knew you better than anyone."

"That isn't true." Although he stopped touching her hair, his gaze was still strong and magnetic, still locked on to hers. "She has no idea what's going on inside of me."

And neither do I, Lea thought. She was never sure what was he thinking, what he was feeling.

He fell silent, and she glanced at the floor, studying the black-and-white tiles. The building still seemed empty, in spite of Cindy being holed up in her office.

"What did she say when you confronted her about leaking the results of the paternity test?" Lea finally asked, resuming their conversation, trying to break the awkward lull.

Michael made a disgusted sound. "She didn't admit it, but she didn't deny it, either. She insulted you, then challenged my evidence, insisting I couldn't prove it."

"Can you?"

"Probably not, but I'm still going to try."

Troubled, Lea sighed. "Have you figured out Cindy's motive?"

"For leaking the information?" He blew out a windy breath. "I think she was trying to push you toward your father and away from me. She wanted you to arrange the press conference, to get closer to your dad. That way you'd go to him when our relationship faltered." He shifted in his seat. "But I don't have any family left. So where would I go?"

She frowned. "To your faithful assistant?"

"Or so she hoped." He reached for her hand. "Do you forgive me, Lea?"

"I already told you that I still love you."

"I know, but that isn't the same as forgiveness." Once again, his gaze locked on to hers. "Is it?"

She wanted to pull away from him, to punish him for her pain, but she couldn't. She could see the truth in his eyes, the remorse, the shame. "We both made mistakes."

"Does that mean you forgive me?"

She kept his hand in hers, wishing his touch didn't leave her aching for more. "Yes."

"Are you sure?"

"Yes," she repeated her answer, moving closer, angling her legs toward his, nearly bumping his knee. He meant everything to her, and he always would. "I won't hold this against you."

"Cindy was a fool to think she could take me away from you." His breath rushed out. "Nobody can replace you. Not in my heart."

Every nerve ending in her body came alive, sizzling beneath her skin, filling her with electricity, with anticipation. "What exactly does that mean?"

"That I finally figured out what love feels like." He grabbed the front of his shirt, as though his heart were racing, pounding rapidly beneath it. "I think deep down I always knew, but I was too afraid to admit it. There was so much turmoil between us. And as soon as Lady Savannah went away, the problem with Cindy started."

Lea's mind started to spin. "You love me?"

He nodded. "Desperately, madly. I've been going

crazy this week without you. But that's how it's been all along. When you're not with me, I can't function." He leaned forward. "But I didn't know that was love. Not until I screwed up. Not until I realized that I'd made all the wrong choices."

"I can't function without you, either." And now she understood why he hadn't been able to clarify his emotions, why being in love confused him.

"Can we start over?" Michael asked.

"Of course we can." She noticed he was still clutching the front of his shirt. "Do you still want me to live with you?"

"More than anything."

"Me, too." Her eyes misted, and he kissed her, brushing her lips with his, giving her the tenderness she craved. She held on to his shoulders, to the strength of his body.

When they separated, they gazed at each other, still caught up in the emotion, in the need to be together.

"It's over," Lea said. "Cindy is out of our lives."

"I can't believe I fell for her ploy. I should have listened to you from the start."

Just then, the door to the offices opened and the blonde strode into the reception area, carrying a small box with her belongings. She looked cool and crisp and a bit too showy, her clothes designed to get her noticed.

"I see you two are talking about me," she said.

"You think?" Michael shot back.

"Jerk," she retorted, her heels sounding on the floor, her skirt hugging her rear.

When she stopped to look at Lea, they glared at

each other. Lea wanted to scratch the other woman eyes out, but only for a second.

By the time Michael's former assistant swept out of the building, she hardly cared.

"Good riddance," he said.

"I'm not as angry as I thought I'd be," Lea admitted.

"How can you say that after what she did to us?"

"Because I'd rather forget that she ever existed."

"So would I." Michael glanced at the door. "But first we have to agree that she's a first-rate bitch."

Lea couldn't help but laugh. "I never said she wasn't a bitch."

He laughed, too. And then he hugged her, holding her close, making the moment last, the incredible feeling of trusting each other, of starting over, of being in love.

John Van Gelder walked among the live oaks at Forsyth Park. He'd spoken to a few people along the way, folks who recognized him and promised him a vote. But that didn't put his mind at ease.

His opponent was still leading in the polls.

Who knew that Abraham's illegitimate child would turn out to be a beautiful Amerasian woman singing her father's praises?

John lifted his shoulders and kept walking, doing his damnedest to appear confident, hoping to make an impression on anyone who saw him.

Didn't it just figure? Only Abraham could engage in an illicit affair and come out of it twenty-eight years later still looking like a war hero.

The son of a bitch had been stricken with amnesia when he'd cheated on his wife. But even so, he'd taken full responsibility, giving the interview of a lifetime.

Once again, Honest Abe had lived up to his name.

Sunlight dappled the walkway and scattered through the trees, making John wish the historic setting would calm his nerves. He loved Savannah. This was his home.

When he looked up, he saw Hayden cut across the path and head toward him. He frowned, wondering why the kid had tracked him down. They hadn't arranged a meeting today.

"Sir?" Hayden approached him, a bit too breathless. The young man looked as though he'd seen a blood-soaked ghost. His skin was pale, his eyes ringed with shadows. "We have a problem."

What now? John thought. How much worse could it get? "I'm listening."

"The woman who helped me was fired from her job. She worked for a security company and the information about the paternity test had come from their files." Hayden's voice vibrated. "Her boss is investigating her."

"That's not our problem."

"What if her boss finds out I was involved?"

John slowed his pace, keeping a safe distance from potential eavesdroppers. "The newspaper isn't going to reveal their source. Her boss isn't going to be able to prove a thing."

"That's what she said." Hayden wouldn't let it go. He shoved his hands in his pockets and exhaled a loud breath. "But it doesn't matter. I can't take this anymore."

"Take what?"

"Digging up dirt on your opponent. I'm turning in my resignation, sir."

John stopped walking, still surrounded by the grandeur of live oaks, still keeping his shoulders back. "Do you think I care? The information you uncovered wasn't worth a plugged nickel. Why didn't that woman tell you the whole story?"

"Maybe she didn't know all the details."

"And maybe she had her own agenda. Maybe you weren't smart enough to see through her."

The kid ignored the insult. "I'm leaving town. I'm going back to Boston. I never liked the South anyway." He rubbed his arm as though a gnat had just bitten him. "I've had enough."

"Then go." John didn't want the little weasel working for him anyway. Anyone who didn't relish Savannah didn't deserve to be part of his campaign. "I'll win this race without you."

Sooner or later, he would come up with another plan to knock Honest Abe off his high-and-mighty pedestal. Because there was no way John was going to settle for less than a seat in the United States Senate.

The wedding was spectacular, the social event of the season. Dusk colored the sky in shades of mauve and blue, and tea lights floated in a lily pond.

The ceremony took place at a Savannah estate, a Greek Revival mansion owned by the bride's family and boasting of old money.

Lea sat with the other guests, watching the procession. Flowers from the formal garden lined the way, making a breathtaking path.

Michael was at the pergola, a limestone structure custom-built for the ceremony. He stood next to the groom, both men wearing black tuxedos.

Clayton Crawford seemed anxious, eager to marry Katrina Beaumont, the woman he called Kat. When the *Bridal March* began, the traditional wedding song seemed to stir his heart. He turned to watch his lady, his expression filled with wonder.

Lea's eyes started to water. Michael watched the bride, too. She captured everyone's attention, with her jeweled gown and cathedral-length veil. She looked like a feminine mystery, the train on her dress trailing gloriously behind her. Her father held her arm, offering her to Clay with a proud nod.

After the vows were spoken and rings exchanged, a pair of white doves were released, followed by a shower of rose petals.

Lea could only imagine how Kat felt, marrying the man she loved, knowing she would spend the rest of her life with him.

An hour later, Lea and Michael sat at the head table at the reception, where she'd been invited to dine with the wedding party since she was Michael's date. She assumed Clay and Kat had made those arrangements, wanting her and Michael to be together.

The ballroom in the mansion was exquisite, with ornate ceilings, stained-glass windows and beveled-glass doors. Trellised balconies offered an expansive view.

A local chef had prepared the meal, and Lea thought the food looked almost too pretty to eat.

Michael reached for his wine. "This is quite an affair, isn't it?"

She nodded and glanced at the bride, wondering if Kat felt like a princess. "A storybook wedding in a Southern castle."

Michael leaned into her. "Is it true that most little girls dream about their weddings? Did you do that when you were young?"

She shook her head. "I tried not to dream too much, but weddings in Vietnam are as important as they are here."

"Tell me what they're like."

His curiosity didn't surprise her. Although she was living with him now, he still asked questions about her culture, wanting her to share bits and pieces of her homeland with him. "The couple who will be married can't see each other on the day before their wedding," she said. "Seeing each other on that day can bring bad luck. Some families don't observe this tradition anymore, but my mother believed in it."

"What else did she believe?" he asked, the flame from a nearby candle reflected in his eyes.

Lea tasted her meal, thinking how handsome he looked in his traditional tuxedo. "She believed the bride's mother should comb her daughter's hair the night before the ceremony."

"Why? Does it mean something special?"

"Yes, especially the third comb. It brings luck and happiness."

He cut into his meat, but he didn't take a bite. He simply held his fork and gazed at her. "I love your hair. It's so pretty, so silky."

She nearly caught her breath. There were hundreds of people all around them, yet somehow it seemed as if they were alone. "In ancient times, a girl's hair was valued, praised in literature, poetry and art. She didn't dare cut it."

"I'm glad you wear yours long." His gaze was still riveted to hers, as though he were memorizing this moment and every word they spoke. "Tell me more about a Vietnamese wedding. What does the bride wear?"

"A traditional bride would wear a dress called *Ao Dai,* and the most appropriate color is red. It represents love and passion."

"What color does the groom wear?"

"Black, with a red flower." She glanced at her plate, at the baked lobster and prime rib, at the seafood-stuffed mushrooms and artfully prepared vegetables. "The food is important, too. There's at least twenty dishes at a Vietnamese wedding, and the egg rolls should come in pairs, so they are like the couple."

"That's nice. Romantic." He smiled at her. "In the old days, when a Seminole girl wanted to find a husband, she draped herself in extra beads and silver ornaments."

"I like that." She returned his smile. "Women adorning themselves for love."

When they both fell silent, one of the bridesmaids engaged them in another conversation and they socialized with everyone at their table, chatting amicably with the wedding party.

The festivities continued, with champagne and cake and a toast from the best man, from Michael. He raised his glass and honored Clay and Kat with humor and warmth, with words that tugged at Lea's heart. Each day that she spent with him, she fell deeper in love, deeper under his spell.

Everyone watched the bride and groom dance, and a bit later Michael and Lea danced, as well. She could smell the woodsy scent of his cologne and the boutonniere pinned to his jacket was the color of fire. Love and passion, she thought.

"I have something for you," he said.

"You do?"

He nodded and led her to the nearest balcony, where they stood in the night air, gazing at the garden below. He reached into his pocket and removed a white gold necklace. "It's a panther."

Awed, she studied the diamond-studded, ruby-eyed cat. "Because you're from the Panther clan?"

"I wanted to give you something that was unique, something special between us."

"It's beautiful." More stunning than anything she'd ever hoped to own.

He moved closer. "It's an engagement gift."

Stunned, Lea lifted her gaze. He was looking at her the way Clay had looked at Kat when he'd watched her walk down the aisle. "Are you asking me to marry you?"

"Yes."

"Oh, my God." She clutched the panther against her heart. "I didn't expect this. Not now, not this soon."

Fear flashed across his face. "Is it too soon?"

"No, not at all." Her eyes misted with tears. "I'd marry you tonight, tomorrow, the next day. I'd become your wife in an instant."

"I don't want to wait, either. We'll do it as quickly as we can." He took her in his arms and stroked a hand down her hair, holding her close. "You're the woman I love, the woman I want to exchange vows with." He stepped back, searching her gaze. "Will you wear a red dress at our wedding?"

"Yes, and I'll wear this, too." She held up the necklace, the jeweled cat shimmering against her skin.

"Let me help you put it on." He moved to stand behind her, then fastened the clasp and brushed his lips against her neck.

She felt her knees go weak, knowing he would have that effect on her for the rest of her life. "I love you, Michael."

"I love you, too." When she faced him again, he touched the panther, then slid his hand a little lower. A simple touch, an erotic touch. Finally he leaned in to kiss her.

He tasted like Cristal, like the French champagne they'd drunk, like the flavor of a fine yet complex bouquet, creating a sensation of creaminess, of white-fleshed fruits and spine-tingling fullness.

"I want to make love," she said.

He smiled against her lips. "Here?"

She smiled, too. "When we get home."

"Then we'll go home soon."

He kissed her again, and she knew she had everything she could want, including the spark that first drew her and Michael together, the beauty of passion, of steamy Savannah nights, of a world only they could create.

\* \* \* \* \*

*Watch for the next book in the*
**DYNASTIES: THE DANFORTHS**
*series with*

*THE ENEMY'S DAUGHTER*

*by Anne Marie Winston,
on sale in September.*

# DYNASTIES: THE DANFORTHS

### A family of prominence...
### tested by scandal, sustained by passion.

# THE ENEMY'S DAUGHTER

## by Anne Marie Winston
### (Silhouette Desire #1603)

Selene Van Gelder and Adam Danforth could not
resist their deep attraction, despite the fact that their
fathers were enemies. When their covert affair was
leaked to the press, they each had to face the truth
about their feelings. Would the feud between their
families keep them apart—or was their love strong
enough to overcome anything?

*Available September 2004 at your favorite retail outlet.*

## Silhouette® Desire®

**Presenting the first book in a new series by**

# Annette Broadrick

## The Crenshaws of Texas

## BRANDED
**(Silhouette Desire #1604)**

When rancher Jake Crenshaw suddenly became
a single dad, he asked Ashley Sullivan to
temporarily care for his daughter. Ashley had
harbored a big childhood crush on Jake and
her feelings were quickly reawakened. Now
Ashley was in Jake's house—and sharing his bed—
but where could this affair of convenience lead…?

*Available September 2004 at your favorite retail outlet.*

If you enjoyed what you just read,
then we've got an offer you can't resist!

# Take 2 bestselling love stories FREE!

# Plus get a FREE surprise gift!

---

**Clip this page and mail it to Silhouette Reader Service™**

**IN U.S.A.**
3010 Walden Ave.
P.O. Box 1867
Buffalo, N.Y. 14240-1867

**IN CANADA**
P.O. Box 609
Fort Erie, Ontario
L2A 5X3

**YES!** Please send me 2 free Silhouette Desire® novels and my free surprise gift. After receiving them, if I don't wish to receive anymore, I can return the shipping statement marked cancel. If I don't cancel, I will receive 6 brand-new novels every month, before they're available in stores! In the U.S.A., bill me at the bargain price of $3.80 plus 25¢ shipping and handling per book and applicable sales tax, if any*. In Canada, bill me at the bargain price of $4.47 plus 25¢ shipping and handling per book and applicable taxes**. That's the complete price and a savings of at least 10% off the cover prices—what a great deal! I understand that accepting the 2 free books and gift places me under no obligation ever to buy any books. I can always return a shipment and cancel at any time. Even if I never buy another book from Silhouette, the 2 free books and gift are mine to keep forever.

225 SDN DZ9F
326 SDN DZ9G

| | | |
|---|---|---|
| Name | (PLEASE PRINT) | |
| Address | Apt.# | |
| City | State/Prov. | Zip/Postal Code |

\* Terms and prices subject to change without notice. Sales tax applicable in N.Y.
\*\* Canadian residents will be charged applicable provincial taxes and GST.
All orders subject to approval. Offer limited to one per household and not valid to current Silhouette Desire® subscribers.
® are registered trademarks owned and used by the trademark owner and or its licensee.

DES04                                    ©2004 Harlequin Enterprises Limited

# COMING NEXT MONTH

### #1603 THE ENEMY'S DAUGHTER—Anne Marie Winston
*Dynasties: The Danforths*
Selene Van Gelder and Adam Danforth could not resist their deep
attraction, despite the fact that their fathers were enemies. When their
covert affair was leaked to the press, they each had to face the truth
about their feelings. Would the feud between their families keep them
apart—or was their love strong enough to overcome anything?

### #1604 BRANDED—Annette Broadrick
*The Crenshaws of Texas*
When rancher Jake Crenshaw suddenly became a single dad, he asked
Ashley Sullivan to temporarily care for his daughter. Ashley had harbored
a big childhood crush on blond-haired Jake and her feelings were quickly
reawakened. Now Ashley was in Jake's house—and sharing his bed—but
where could this affair of convenience lead…?

### #1605 MEETING AT MIDNIGHT—Eileen Wilks
*Mantalk*
Mysterious Seely Jones immediately mesmerized Ben McClain. He tried
his best to pry into her deep, dark secrets but Seely held on tight to what
he wanted. Ben kept up his hot pursuit, but would what he sought fan his
flaming desire or extinguish his passion?

### #1606 UNMASKING THE MAVERICK PRINCE—Kristi Gold
*The Royal Wager*
Never one for matrimony, Mitchell Edward Warner III didn't expect to
lose a wager that he wouldn't marry for ten years. But when journalist
Victoria Barnet set her sights on convincing blue-eyed Mitch to take his
vows in exchange for a lifetime of passionate, wedded bliss, this sexy
son of a senator started to reconsider….

### #1607 A BED OF SAND—Laura Wright
Neither Rita Thompson nor her gorgeous boss, Sheikh Sakir Ibn Yousef
Al-Nayhal, meant for their mock marriage to go beyond business. She
needed a groom to reunite her family, and he needed a bride to return to
his homeland. Yet fictitious love soon turned into real passion and Rita
couldn't resist her tall, dark and handsome desert prince.

### #1608 THE FIRE STILL BURNS—Roxanne St. Claire
Competing architects Colin McGrath and Grace Harrington came from
two different worlds. But when forced into close quarters for a design
competition, it was more than blueprints that evoked their passion, and
pretty soon Grace found herself falling for her hot and sexy rival….

SDCNM0804